The Face of the Foe

PATRICIA POWER

PUBLISHED FOR THE CRIME CLUB BY
DOUBLEDAY & COMPANY, INC., GARDEN CITY, NEW YORK
1973

All of the characters in this book are fictitious, and any resemblance to actual persons, living or dead, is purely coincidental.

ISBN: 0-385-03669-8
Library of Congress Catalog Card Number 72–94758
Copyright © 1973 by Patricia Power
All Rights Reserved
Printed in the United States of America
First Edition

The Face of the Foe

Chapter 1

I'd almost forgotten about my encounter at the mailbox last night with T. Oliphant when Laura mentioned him at dinner on a Friday night in late November.

"Have you noticed anything odd about that man with the thick glasses who moved into Apartment 4 about a month ago?"

"Decidedly yes! I've seen him half a dozen times, but last night was the first time I came face to face with him. We happened to arrive at the mailbox at the same time. He gave me a look that sent shivers through me then his eyes slid away and he pursed his lips as though he'd encountered something disgusting."

Laura nodded. "I met him at the door tonight and got about the same treatment. Maybe it's those thick lenses, but his eyes had a glittery brilliance about them that made him look sinister. He glared at me a moment and his mouth tightened up as though something distasteful had come within his line of vision. Then he walked into the inner lobby—letting the door close in my face!"

The man we were discussing—I'd gotten his name from the mailbox in the lobby—was a tall, stooped, cadaverous-looking creature with a bald, high-domed head and a grayish coloring that could best be described with the words "prison pallor." On every occasion I'd met him in the building, coming or going, he'd averted his gaze and given me a wide berth. Last night was the first time I'd seen him really close up and I hoped I wouldn't repeat the experience for a while.

"Maybe," said Laura, breaking the crust of her Streusel raisin loaf, "he just doesn't like women."

"You could be right there. He certainly *looked* at me as though he hated me—almost as though he'd like to *murder* me!"

"He gave me the same feeling, Nicky. I wonder what he does for a living. Probably some unpleasant job like undertaker or gravedigger."

"Well, if you can believe Sybil Hepworth—which is asking a lot, I know—he makes bombs."

"Bombs!" exclaimed my apartmentmate, choking on a mouthful of her dessert. "Where on earth did she get that idea?"

"Where does Sybil get *any* of her ideas? It's elementary, according to her. He doesn't seem to have a job; is home most of the time; Sybil hears mysterious hammering noises coming from his apartment all day. Can't you see her crouched at the keyhole of his apartment with her ear cocked? When he does go out, he's always carrying a brown carton—a freshly made bomb, what else?"

Laura threw back her lustrous red head and laughed. "Leave it to Miss Hepworth to make cloak-and-dagger stuff out of some innocent hammering and brown packages. She loves drama. Come to think of it, though, the few times I've seen Oliphant leave the building on a Saturday when I was coming in, he *was* carrying a brown carton."

"And every time I've passed him going out on the weekend, he was toting a brown box. What do you suppose could be in them? Shrunken heads?"

"Sybil would love that! Much better than bombs!"

Sybil Hepworth, a pudgy middle-aged spinster with dyed

2

red hair, small malicious eyes, and a blotched, pasty complexion, is the apartment building's snoop, gossip and troublemaker. From her vantage point in Apartment 2, directly across the hall from us, Sybil can spy on our comings and goings to her mean little heart's content. And she does, she does. Laura and I have gotten used to glancing across the hall as we bid goodnight to friends at the door just in time to see Sybil's door silently opening—or closing. It's one of the minor irritations of living at 5931 Phoebe Lane, but considering the advantages of living there, it isn't worth a second thought. Phoebe Lane is a short, one-way street off Winnicott Road, bounded at the other end by a tree-bordered lane, and 5931 is an older apartment building, sedate and undistinguished on the outside but full of delightful surprises on the inside. Like big, really big, high-ceilinged rooms, parquetry flooring throughout, a brick fireplace in the living room and oodles of cupboard space. It's Laura's apartment; I've been sharing it with her for a year and consider the day I answered her advertisement in the Apartments to Share column a red-letter day.

"More raisin loaf, Nicky?"

I brought myself back to the present and shook my head. "No thanks, friend, it's delicious—like everything you make —but fattening. I'll have some more coffee though."

Laura talked while she poured coffee for us. "To change the subject from unpleasant personalities to pleasant ones, what do you think of Till Eulenspiegel for a name for the restaurant?"

"Till Eulenspiegel," I said blankly. "Someone I should know?"

"I should hope not. He's dead."

So he was pleasant but he was dead. "Tell me more," I said, fascinated by the turn the conversation was taking. Laura lit a cigarette and blew a spiral of smoke in my direction.

"Teutonic. Born circa 1300 and the subject of a collection

3

of satirical tales published in 1515. Till Eulenspiegel was a scapegrace, notorious for playing tricks on the Establishment —innkeepers not excepted. Don't you think it would be a great name for my restaurant? When customers raise their beer steins, the ghost of Till Eulenspiegel will be capering about the place looking for fresh mischief to get into. It ties in with the whole idea of fun and frolic I'm trying to create for my beer garden."

"Well, now that I know what you're talking about, it does sound great for a beer garden. But how many of your customers will know who the gentleman under discussion is?"

"That's no problem, Nicky. The legend of Till Eulenspiegel will be proclaimed on a plaque outside the restaurant and on every menu. In no time at all, *everybody* will know Till Eulenspiegel."

Laura propped her elbows on the table, rested her chin on her hands and gave me her gamin grin. I grinned back in admiration. I had to hand it to Laura Prescott. She has imagination and brains. If anyone could make a success of a Bavarian beer garden, it was Laura. Right now she's a dietician for Harrington Flour Mills and a wizard with a stove, but she's got her heart set on her own restaurant and has been making plans for months. It's a dream she's had for years, but there was the slight problem of financing until Laura's mother, Cecci Damrosch, suddenly turned into Lady Bountiful and solved the money problem. It all came about because of the Roman Spring of Mrs. Damrosch. Laura's mother—who's as kooky as they come—had a high-fashion boutique on elegant Sherbrooke Street—and an elegant clientele to match. She made three or four trips a year to Rome to buy Italian fashions and last spring in Rome Cecci succumbed to the charms of Bernardo Antonelli, Italian fashion designer. He wooed and won her and it was agreed they would make beautiful fashions together in Rome. Cecci flew home to Montreal, sold her boutique and, in the glow and good will produced by her late-blooming romance, presented Laura with a hefty share of

4

the sale, before flying back to Rome to take up residence as Mrs. Bernardo Antonelli. Laura, as elated as her mother, stashed the fifty-thousand-dollar bonanza in the bank, along with the six thousand she'd already saved, and set enthusiastically to work to make her dream come true. For months now she's been experimenting with German cookery, collecting antique beer steins, searching for a property and a partner. This fall she enrolled in a course in restaurant administration at the Drummond Business Institute.

I glanced across the table at Laura—into sea-foam green eyes set in a small, heart-shaped face lightly dusted with freckles. Setting off the winsome face was a shoulder-length fall of coppery red hair that made Laura a real traffic stopper.

"Has that woman at the school come to any decision about going into the restaurant with you, Laura?"

"Yes. As a matter of fact, she told me just last night that she'd like to go in with me. And I'm pretty excited about it. Claire St.-Germaine hasn't as much money to put into the business as I'd like—she'll be the junior partner—but she's had twelve years' experience cooking for hospitals and restaurants and is a great cook. She'll be head chef and I'll do a little of everything until we can afford enough help to keep things running smoothly. We're planning on getting some students from the university to serve as barmaids—blond, Nordic types if we can get them. And there has to be music of course. Eventually we hope to be able to pay for a Bavarian-style band, but for a starter we're looking for an accordionist with a good repertoire of German folk songs and beer songs."

"Hey, it sounds like it's really going to swing!"

Laura set her coffee cup down decisively. "If schmaltz is swingy, it will swing, Nicky. Bavarian baroque decor, window box geraniums, folk costumes on the girls—the whole bit. And last—and most important—good food and good beer, at a reasonable price. That will bring them back for more. Claire and I are getting together tomorrow night to work out some menus. We'll each experiment with recipes to work out the basic costs of producing them in quantity. Then we can decide which items we'll feature. And I almost forgot to tell you. I got an answer to my ad for a property. It's a delicatessen-restaurant with modern equipment. The owner's retiring. And the location is almost too good to be true. On Decelles right across from the University of Montreal, so I'd get all the university students. The owner was a real chatty type and I found myself telling him all about my plans and my course in Restaurant Administration at the Drummond Business Institute. It turned out he has a friend taking the course there. He seemed so interested in everything and even gave me advice on food preparation and ways to cut costs. He said with the capital I had to invest I shouldn't have any trouble swinging it."

"It sounds like the perfect spot for a beer garden. When are you going to see the place?"

"Tomorrow at three. I'm just hoping it's as good as it sounds and won't need too many renovations. When the location's that ideal, there's bound to be something else that's not right. It would be funny if I found a place on my own when that real estate agent has been searching for me in vain for three months."

Laura stubbed out her cigarette and got up from the table. "I can hardly wait until tomorrow, but right now I'd better stop talking and get moving. Amy and I are going to a movie and we want to make the early show."

I got up too and stretched. "I don't envy you going out on a blustery night like tonight. I'm going to curl up with a good book after I do the dishes."

It was my week for dishwashing. Laura and I had it worked out nicely. One week she did the shopping for food, prepared the meals and served them and I did the cleaning up. The next week we reversed the procedure. The other household chores were all fairly apportioned in the same way, so there was no room for friction on the division of labor.

I'd finished the dishes and was wiping off the Dutch-tile countertop when Laura stopped in the kitchen doorway to say goodbye. Tall and slim, she looked like a model in her white suede maxi-coat with red fox trim, white boots and white Cossack-style fur hat. Why, I wondered, was a girl who looked like *that* going to a movie with a *girl* on a Friday night!

I hung up the dish towel, fetched an Elizabeth Kent novel from my bed-sitting room and prepared to spend a cozy evening reading in the living room. The room was a little chilly and I decided a fire would make it cosier. When I had a crackling wood fire going in the white brick fireplace, I settled down with my book on one of Laura's big, cushiony sofas.

For a few minutes I just sat listening to the wind rush past the living room windows and the French doors leading to the little terrace—another fringe benefit of 5931 Phoebe Lane. All our rooms faced on the lane and in the summer we dined alfresco, shaded from the heat by the big trees that overhung the terrace. And it seemed to me that most of last summer's weekend lunches on the terrace had consisted of *Weck, Wurst* and *Wein*—or roll, sausage, and wine, if you're not up on your German. Laura had gone Teutonic in a big way since she'd decided to open her beer garden—and influenced me accordingly. Not that I'm complaining. Laura's German dishes add zest and variety to our meals and since she's such a good cook, anything she makes is bound to be good.

I couldn't help but wonder why there were no men in Laura's life. She'd been having a heavy romance with a young stockbroker when I'd moved in a year ago, but four months later it suddenly went kaput. Laura never talked about it and I'm not one to ask questions, so I don't know what happened, but I had the feeling that it was Carl who'd ended the affair, because Laura went around in a fog for months, seemingly well lost to the world. By the summer she'd rallied and decided to join the world again. Since then there'd been an occasional date with a personable-looking man, but they never seemed to come to anything. I had the feeling that my apartmentmate had been badly burned in that romance that went up in smoke and had donned a cloak

7

of aloofness with the male sex to avoid getting singed again. At any rate, regardless of what she was doing or not doing, she was keeping the men at bay. What a waste of a girl who had so much to offer. Just looking around her living room, you knew here was a girl with flair and youth and gaiety. The big room sparkled with color, keyed by the gay cotton prints of warm goldenrod, bright green and white on the sofas. Vibrant flower still lifes splashed color on the white walls, and green wrought-iron cages filled with greenery created the effect of an outdoor bower. Hard to believe, in Laura's garden-like living room, that outside, the temperature was a frigid ten degrees and a gusty wind howled through the leafless trees.

A moaning tree branch suddenly cracked against the French doors and I got up and drew the draperies. What miserable weather and worse to come—sleet, snow and bone-chilling cold. But I wasn't too concerned. In just two weeks I'd be winging my way to the Caribbean on my Christmas holidays. That was *the* big advantage of being secretary to the principal of a girls' school. Holidays. A full two months in the summer, two and a half weeks at Christmas, *plus* a generous number of days off for teachers' conferences, special school events, etc. It more than made up for the boredom of working in a girls' school, surrounded by coltish adolescents with braces on their teeth, and prim and proper British teachers in tweedy suits and sensible shoes—and not a man in sight! But one must take the bitter with the sweet, and those long vacations *were* sweet. In the two years I'd worked at Kensington School for Girls, I'd had a two-week-long Christmas holiday in Martinique and another in Acapulco; seven wonderful weeks in Greece during the first summer I was at the school, and six roving weeks in Spain the summer past. The school closed for Christmas holidays December 17, but this year I'd be leaving on December 10. The former principal, Miss Redgrave, had died suddenly last summer, two weeks before school was to reopen in September, and the new replacement, Miss Eden, has asked me to cut my vacation a little short to

8

help her get oriented and organized in her new position. I'd just arrived home from Spain the weekend before and eagerly went back to work early when Miss Eden promised me an extra week at Christmas to make up. So on December 11, I'd be on my way to Jamaica. Between rum punches on the beach, I intended to spare a thought now and then for my less fortunate friends in frigid Montreal.

Happy in the prospect of bliss to come, I curled up comfortably on the sofa, picked up my book and started reading.

Chapter 2

By the time I reached the cliff-hanging part of my murder mystery, the creaking of branches in the wind and the crackling of the fire had faded into the background of consciousness. I was so deeply absorbed in my story that the sudden, frantic pounding at the door made me leap wildly in fright, hurling my book in the air.

I rushed through the living room into the front entrance hall and paused uncertainly. Who could it be and what was wrong? No one had rung the buzzer. I was almost afraid to open the door, but the urgent hammering went on like a cry for help and I could hesitate no longer. I unlocked and opened the door a crack, my heart skipping wildly.

The white, terrified face of a woman looked into mine. "Please, please let me in! Someone's after me!"

I couldn't disregard a plea like that. Quickly I took the chain off and swung the door wide. The woman rushed into the foyer, bumping into me in her haste to get inside. Hur-

9

riedly I closed the door and slid the chain into place, fearful that her pursuer might be right behind.

"Oh, thank you, thank you," she said, gasping for breath. "He was right behind me all the way down Winnicott—then he was right *beside* me and—" She stopped, clutching nervously at her throat.

The woman was so agitated I thought it useless to ask questions until I'd gotten her quieted down. "You're safe now," I said in a matter-of-fact tone to calm her. Taking her arm, I led her into the living room and over to one of the sofas.

"Just sit down and rest for a few minutes. I'm going to give you something to drink that will make you feel better. Then you can tell me about it."

She sat down heavily on the sofa, depositing an armful of sheet music and books on the coffee table in front of her with shaking hands.

I went out to the kitchen and poured a generous measure of brandy into a glass, noting that it was ten-thirty by my watch. As I returned to the living room with the drink a sudden shiver of fear ran down my spine. I'd just remembered that only four nights ago a woman had been found strangled inside a garage on Winnicott Road.

"Drink this down," I said with a firmness I was suddenly far from feeling. "Then we'll talk."

I watched her as she drank the brandy. A big, ungainly-looking woman with a round childlike face framed by black sausage curls. About thirty-eight or thereabouts, and well-to-do, judging by the pastel mink coat and velvet pants she was wearing. She drank the brandy too fast and coughed and sputtered as it burned its way down. Her hands were still trembling. I waited until she had finished, then sat down beside her, prepared to find out what was going on. She played nervously with the pearl necklace at her throat, but her fear-contorted features had smoothed out, leaving her with the wistful, anxious expression of a lost child.

10

"Now, tell me about it. First of all, what's your name and how did you get in without ringing the buzzer?"

"I'm Kathleen Windsor. I didn't have to ring the buzzer. The inner lobby door wasn't locked." Her voice was high-pitched and shrill, incongruous with her big frame. That damn door. The spring mechanism on the lock was broken and the janitor had promised to have it fixed but still hadn't gotten around to it. *Anybody* could walk in!

"I'm Nicole Nugent. You said somebody was after you?"

"Yes," she said, and her big eyes went round with fear again. "He followed me along Côte St. Luc from Girouard and then down Winnicott. I crossed the street and a minute later he crossed right behind me. He was getting closer and closer behind me and I was so frightened, oh, so frightened." Her little-girl voice went so high it squeaked. "I live on Winnicott, close to Queen Mary, but I knew he'd pounce on me before I could reach home. I could feel him breathing down my neck. And I *knew* he was going to pounce any second and I didn't know what to do. Then, suddenly, he was right *beside* me and I rushed down Phoebe Lane. I know it's a dead-end street, but I was too frightened to think. Your building was the last one on the street and I ran into it and pounded on your door." She ended her dramatic recital a little out of breath and peered anxiously into the foyer as though she expected the man who had followed her to materialize in the doorway.

"You're safe now," I reassured her. "The door's locked."

"Yes," she said in a frightened voice, "but what will happen when I leave? Just Monday night a girl from my church choir was murdered on Winnicott."

So Elsie Grunberger had sung in the same choir as Kathleen. No wonder she was frightened.

"Did the man say anything to you, Kathleen?"

"He muttered something, but I couldn't understand. I'm so thankful to be here." Her voice had dropped an octave or two

11

and her hands had stopped fidgeting with her necklace. The brandy had taken effect.

"Did you see what he looked like?" I asked.

"I didn't get a clear look. I glanced at him when he was on the other side of the street. He was wearing a dark coat and he was short and sinister-looking. When he got right beside me I didn't *dare* look!"

I debated calling the police but wondered if there was any point to it. On any given night in a big city probably a dozen women were followed and accosted on the street. And after the woman had rushed into my building the man had no doubt cleared out of the area in a hurry. Furthermore, she didn't even have a description of him. She couldn't see him clearly across the street in the dark. Certainly not clearly enough to judge whether or not he was "sinister-looking." But again I thought of that woman who'd been murdered one block over from me.

"Would you like me to call the police, Kathleen?"

"Oh no." Her voice was shrill again. "They'd ask a lot of questions and mother would be *sure* to hear about it. Choir practice is over at nine-thirty and mother likes me to come straight home. She'd be so angry!" Kathleen Windsor looked at me anxiously with her big please-like-me blue eyes. Her voice dropped suddenly and she whispered in a conspiratorial tone, "Mother's in the hospital right now, so I stayed late at church talking to one of the choir members." She giggled at the end of this admission, as pleased and scared as a child who has defied authority.

My God, what have we here? I thought, and a sudden suspicion dawned. Was this immature woman, with her dramatic recital of being followed, imagining things? Was she akin to the spinster who kept looking nervously under the bed for fear of finding a man there? Had the man *actually* followed her and said something to her or had wishful thinking made her believe so? I thought about it for a minute and decided against calling the police. Even if Kathleen Windsor's story

12

were substantially true, there was nothing the police could do now and she didn't want me to call them. But just to be on the safe side, I was going to see that the woman got home okay.

"Is there anyone at home with you, Kathleen?"

"No, I'm all alone. And I'm afraid to go home. He may be out there waiting for me."

I could have called a taxi, but I felt a responsibility for this wistful, strangely childlike woman. I was going to see her safely inside her apartment myself. And then I had an unpleasant thought. If I walked Kathleen Windsor home I'd have to come back alone. And supposing that a man *had* followed her and was still lingering about? The murder so close to home had unnerved me more than I cared to admit. If Laura were home she'd come with us and there'd be two of us coming back to Phoebe Lane. She should be home soon. But then she might have decided to go to Amy's place after the movie. Suddenly I thought of the janitor. George Matrai was a quiet, good-natured little man and he'd told me he liked to take walks at night. If he was home maybe he wouldn't mind walking to Kathleen's apartment with me.

"I'm going to walk home with you, Kathleen, and I'm going to see if Mr. Matrai—the janitor here—will go with us."

"Oh, thank you so much. I'd be *terrified* to go home alone now. But I'm sorry to be such a bother." Kathleen Windsor hung her head apologetically as though she'd been guilty of being a bother on too many occasions.

"It's no trouble, Kathleen. I'll try and get Mr. Matrai on the phone."

George Matrai was home and when I explained the situation on the phone, he willingly agreed to walk to Kathleen's apartment with me.

A few minutes later there was a gentle knock on my door and this time I wasn't afraid to open it. I'd gotten my coat and boots on, so we were all ready to leave. Kathleen giggled unexpectedly when I introduced her to the janitor. His broad,

13

swarthy face assumed a puzzled expression; then he politely made his face go blank. Mr. Matrai is a very polite man.

We were almost at the front door when I remembered that Kathleen had been carrying some music and books when she arrived and she didn't have them now. So we went back, Kathleen retrieved her belongings and we were on our way again. Sybil Hepworth's door closed silently as we came out of the apartment the second time. And we met T. Oliphant coming in. He looked at us with that strange glittery glare; then his eyes traveled down Kathleen Windsor's mink to her knees. His mouth pursed up and he swung over to the opposite side of the hall. The man was decidedly odd.

"What number are you at on Winnicott?" I asked Kathleen.

"Forty-nine hundred. Seabury House."

I'd passed it often enough. An ultra-plush, ultra-expensive new building a little below Queen Mary. It went with the mink Kathleen was wearing.

A cold blast of air hit us as Mr. Matrai opened the outer door and we stepped into the night, Kathleen guarded by me on one side and pudgy Mr. Matrai on the other, no taller than herself. A full moon rode high behind a veil of clouds, and the barren boughs of trees swayed drunkenly in the wind. We walked quickly, heads down against the tearing wind, and arrived at Seabury House in three minutes flat.

A doorman in maroon and gold livery swung the outer door open for us, tipped his peaked hat to Kathleen, then admitted us into the inner sanctum—all marble and glass and Grecian-looking pillars. We rode a whispery-silent paneled elevator to the fourth floor, walked down a thickly carpeted, softly lit hall and stopped in front of a plum-colored door with the number 415 on it. We waited while Kathleen searched her purse for her keys, found them and opened the door.

"It was so good of you to bring me home, Miss Nugent and Mr. Matrai." Kathleen giggled when she looked at George Matrai. "Won't you please come in for a minute? Just to see

14

that everything's all right," she added anxiously. "He might have gotten into my apartment somehow." The childlike blue eyes were big with anticipated danger.

How her pursuer, if such he were, could have gotten past the doorman and into her apartment without a key was beyond me. Kathleen Windsor *did* have an imagination. And I wasn't about to argue with it. The only thing to do was go in and check and then, hopefully, she would be reassured.

George looked at me impassively, but I had the feeling he had formed the same impression of the woman as I had. He nodded obligingly at Kathleen, and we were ushered through a room-size foyer into a huge living room hung in heavy gold velvet, with a velvety-piled rug to match. The furniture was all a pale, polished brown and looked French in design. The mink went with money, all right, I thought, mentally figuring the cost of furnishing this big room in such opulent style.

Kathleen asked George to go through the apartment, room by room, and check all the cupboards and the window leading to the fire escape. So George, with Kathleen and me trailing in his wake, obediently trotted from room to room, peering into cupboards and behind doors. The last room in our search for an intruder was Kathleen's and it reinforced my image of her as a child who had never grown up. A little girl's room, all pink and white, with ruffled curtains and bedspread and a menagerie of plush animals on the big four-poster. A huge pink Teddy bear with glass-button eyes stared at me from a rocking chair while the janitor conducted his search of the room. He closed a cupboard door behind him and spoke to Kathleen.

"Nothing, miss, there's nobody here."

"Would you just look under the bed, Mr. Matrai? He might be hiding under the bed."

I knew she would giggle and she did. George looked at me and one eyebrow went up. I had a sudden urge to giggle myself but controlled it. George, his face still impassive, got down on hands and knees and peered under the organdy spread. I was almost convinced now that Kathleen Windsor had not been followed at all. The man had been walking behind her simply because his route home was the same as hers. When he came up beside her, he was likely just passing her, and Kathleen, her imagination running riot, had imagined he'd spoken to her and was about to grab her. Laura would have a good laugh when I told her about it.

George straightened up and spoke firmly. "There is nothing to worry about, miss. No one is hiding in the apartment."

There was an expression of infinite relief on Kathleen's face. She led us back to the front of the apartment. When we reached the foyer she hesitated, looked around nervously as though unseen eyes were watching her, then asked timidly in her shrill, little-girl voice, "Would you like a glass of sherry?" Somehow I had the idea that her mother wouldn't approve of her drinking sherry with strangers and that Kathleen was being a bad girl again.

George shook his head and I followed suit. "No thanks, Kathleen, we'll be on our way. We just wanted to make sure you got home safely."

She thanked us again profusely and said if there was ever anything she could do for us to please, please let her know. And then we were out in the cold again, hurrying down the deserted windy street, George apparently too overcome by his experience to say anything at all. We parted outside my door and I let myself into the apartment, a little overcome myself by my meeting with Miss Windsor. It was five to eleven.

I found Laura in the kitchen putting coffee on to perk. I told her the whole story over coffee and cake and Laura agreed that the woman was probably imagining things.

And here I'd left my warm fire and my book to protect a woman from a nonexistent pursuer. In the future I'd confine my girl scout activities to the daytime. One consolation: The walk in the cold was probably good for my circulation.

16

Chapter 3

I woke early on Saturday with the top of my head throbbing gently and painfully. And after I'd gotten up, moved around a bit and thoroughly wakened myself, I made additional painful discoveries. My nose was stuffy, my throat hurt and little gremlins were jabbing sharp needles deep into my bones. And I had a dinner date with Chris tonight. Great! Just great! But I consoled myself with the thought that two weeks from today I'd be soaking up warmth on my island in the sun, where nobody had so much as *heard* of a cold!

I went into the bathroom, took two aspirin and went back to bed. When I wakened again it was almost noon. Reluctantly I dragged my aching bones out of bed, put on a housecoat and went in search of food. The aspirin had stopped the throbbing in my head, but I still felt like somebody's revenge. I'd have to give Chris a rain check on our date for tonight.

In the kitchen Laura was breaking eggs for an omelet and there was a whiff of onion soup in the air. I greeted her dolefully in a raspy voice. "Nice morning if you like mornings."

Laura, fresh-faced and gay in a yellow-flowered duster, gave me a long look from wide sea-green eyes. "It's not too hard to guess you have a cold, Nicky. Tough luck. Have you eaten anything this morning?"

"No, I woke up early but went back to bed."

"I just got up myself. I'll make enough omelet for both of us."

"Soup's all I want, Laura. I'm not hungry."

17

"Eat the omelet like a good girl. I'm putting chicken in it—lots of protein. Good for you. You don't want to be sick when your vacation comes up."

That was the dietician talking and she was probably right, so I dutifully ate a large portion of chicken omelet when it was ready. While we ate, Laura talked about the restaurant she was going to see that afternoon, speculating whether it would be suitable for her purpose. Then I brought up the subject of Kathleen Windsor again and tried to give Laura a clear picture of how incredibly childish the woman was.

"I'd take her to be about thirty-eight, but she acts about eight. Would you believe she didn't want me to call the police for fear her mother would get to hear of it? Right now her mother's in the hospital and Kathleen's being naughty. She's supposed to come straight home from choir practice at nine-thirty, and here she stayed late talking to somebody and didn't reach my place until ten-thirty. 'Mother would be so angry!' " I mimicked Kathleen's shrill, childish voice.

"She does sound sort of unbelievable, but it takes all kinds to make a world. You wouldn't have felt right if you hadn't taken her home last night."

"You're right, Laura. She looked like she needed somebody to take charge. And I'd still be worrying if I hadn't seen her safely home."

After lunch, Laura went out to get our grocery order for the week. I took another two aspirin, washed the dishes and wandered aimlessly around, feeling too miserable to know what to do with myself but not wanting to go to bed. Finally I decided to die with my boots on and dressed in warm corduroy pants and a thick sweater. But I still felt shivery. It was another cold day and the apartment was always a little on the chilly side when the temperature dropped below ten degrees.

At a quarter to two I went out to get our mail, which, as usual, was mostly bills and circulars. I'd just gotten back to our apartment door when Sybil Hepworth's door opened and she waddled importantly across the hall toward me, larger than life in a quilted orange robe.

"Good morning, Miss Nugent. It's a cold day, isn't it?"

The weather was always Sybil's opening gambit. Then she got down to business, her voice dropping to a confidential whisper. "You know that Cynthia Allen in Apartment 12?"

I didn't know Cynthia Allen in Apartment 12, but that didn't make any difference to Miss Hepworth. She had some dirt to unload and she was going to unload it. On she went without waiting for an answer to her question.

"She came in at three o'clock this morning—with a man! So drunk he was holding her up. And he went upstairs to her apartment with her!" Sybil's malicious little eyes, drowning in puffs of fat, gleamed with pleasurable shock. "Imagine! Bold-facedly coming in in that condition and letting him go up to her apartment. And her no more than a child! We shouldn't have to put up with goings-on like that in a respectable building. I'm going to report it to the owner. And just last Thursday she was parading in the laundry room wearing—"

I cut out Sybil's voice with a sharp-tongued retort. "Why not wait until Monday to report her, Miss Hepworth? Sundays she comes in drunk at three A.M.—with two men!" Then I closed my apartment door firmly in her face. At the best of times Sybil Hepworth was hard to take. Achy and miserable as I felt, she was impossible. And I'd long ago reached the conclusion that Sybil moved her bed out to the lobby at bedtime. How else would she know about all the scandalous comings and goings in the hall in the middle of the night?

Back in the apartment, I dropped our mail on the kitchen table without bothering to open mine and dully decided I'd better call Chris and give him the bad news. He was going to be disappointed. But when I phoned, there was no answer. It would have to wait until Chris called me. A few minutes later Laura returned from her shopping trip and half an hour later she was gone to see the property near the University of Montreal. I lit a fire in the living room to warm my aching bones and curled up on a sofa with a blanket over me. But despite the fire and the blanket I lay shivering until I fell asleep.

The closing of the front door wakened me and I sat up groggily, ready to hear Laura's report of the restaurant she'd visited. She came into the living room, still wearing her coat and hat, plunked a paper down on the coffee table with unnecessary force and slumped onto the sofa beside me.

"It wasn't what you were looking for?" It was really a statement, not a question. Laura was not wearing the face that goes with a happy outcome.

"It was *exactly* what I was looking for. Nice-looking building, beautiful location, a big area on one side of the building that would be perfect for the beer garden in the summer."

"Then what was wrong?" I asked, puzzled by the grim set of Laura's face and the stormy look in the usually serene green eyes.

"What was wrong was that it wasn't for sale!" Laura's tone was pure acid.

"Wasn't for sale?" I repeated, more puzzled than ever.

"Right, Nicky. It wasn't for sale. At first I didn't know which one of us was crazy. I told the owner he *called* me and we *discussed* it. But it was news to him. He said somebody must have been playing a joke on me. Joke! If I could get my hands on that—"

"A hoax? But that doesn't make sense. You said the man was so interested . . . he was giving you advice on the business—"

"*Somebody* was giving me advice—but it wasn't the owner of Lou's Delicatessen. And don't ask me to explain the workings of a joker's mind. I guess it was a mistake to put my own advertisement in the paper. Live and learn. Who's got time to run around looking at mythical properties for sale? I'm going to let the real estate agent take it from here." Laura

20

got up dejectedly. "I'm going to make myself a drink. Do you want a hot rum? Might make you feel better."

"Yes. And make it mostly rum. I'm so cold I don't think I'll ever get warm again, but it's worth a try."

While Laura was fixing the drinks the phone rang and I got up to answer it. It was probably Chris.

"Hello, Muffet, all set for tonight?"

It was a term of endearment with Chris, but there was sometimes a faintly amused tone in the quiet, deep voice when he addressed me as "Muffet." Someday I was going to ask him what was funny.

"I'm sorry to disappoint you, Chris, but I'm not going to be able to go out tonight. I've got a thrice-lousy cold and the way I'm shivering I think it's going to develop into pneumonia. For me, it's home and fireside tonight."

His tone changed from amused to sympathetic. "Poor Muffet, you don't sound so good. And here we were really going to dine in style on a royalty check that arrived yesterday. Never mind, it'll be twice as good next week. Is Laura going to be home tonight?"

"No, she's going out for dinner."

"Well, what if I bring some Chinese food and keep you company for dinner, or do you feel too miserable to see me?"

I considered my unfortunate condition for a moment, then decided to answer in the affirmative. A visit with Chris would take my mind off present afflictions for a little while anyway and shorten this miserable day.

"I'm good for a few hours I think, Chris. I'd like it if you came down for a while. But please don't stay late. The flag's really flying at half-mast and I'm going to bed early."

"Just an hour or two to boost your morale. Then I'll be on my way. Will seven be okay?"

"Yes, Chris, I'll be waiting for you."

I hung up the phone and went back to my resting place and blanket. My drink was on the square yellow table in

21

front of the sofa. Laura was sipping hers at the big desk in front of the windows.

"That Chris, Nicky?"

"Yes, he's coming down for a little while and bringing food with him. What time are you going to Claire's place for dinner?"

"I'll be going out about five-thirty. Right now I'm trying to pick out the most likely recipes for menus from my files and Claire's doing the same thing. Tonight we'll decide which recipes to experiment with. But I've got so many it's hard to choose."

I could see the problem. Laura had three recipe boxes in front of her and several thick folders, all filled with recipes. I looked around the room with a heavy eye.

"I'd have made a stab at doing the vacuuming and cleaning up if I'd known Chris was going to come down tonight. Now I haven't got the strength."

"Don't worry about it, Nicky. If it's love, a little disorder won't kill it. I'll do your chores tomorrow when I have more time."

Laura went back to her work and I sipped my drink slowly, gazing dully at the leaping fire. She'd made my drink strong all right and in no time I was sleepy. I curled up again, pulled the blanket over me and shivered my way to sleep. The glass-button eyes of a big plush Teddy bear stared at me reproachfully until I drifted into oblivion.

Chapter 4

When I awakened the room was in shadow and the fire had died to a red glow. I got up, switched on the lights and looked at my watch. Quarter to six. The apartment was silent. Laura would have left by now.

I decided against getting dressed for Chris's visit. Warm clothes were what I needed in my present condition and my corduroys and cable-knit sweater were the warmest clothes I owned. But I could do something about my face. I marched off to the bathroom and took a look in the mirror. Rouge would conceal the pallor of my complexion and a little judiciously applied eye make-up would play down the lackluster look in my eyes.

After I'd finished with the make-up I turned my attention to my hair. It's black, when I would have liked it to be blond or coppery red like Laura's, but at least it's black black, not charcoal gray or mousy black. I wear it in a short, swinging page boy with a fringe of hair across my forehead. When he isn't calling me Muffet or Nicky, Chris calls me the Egyptian or Cleopatra, because of my hair style. When he's annoyed with me he calls me Nicole. I brushed my hair vigorously until I'd worked up a gleam in it and decided I'd done all I could for the cause.

Back to the living room and my security blanket, after first heaping the fire with wood and waiting till the flames winged, indigo-tipped, over the top of the fire screen. There was nearly an hour to go before Chris arrived. I snuggled up shivering in my blanket and dreamily watched the fire, thinking of Chris.

23

There was a lot to think about. He'd asked me to marry him twice now and I wondered how long it would be before he lost patience and turned his attentions elsewhere. I was losing patience with myself for my dithering, but I couldn't seem to come to a decision.

Marriage. For me it was a giant step. And I wanted to jump into it with both feet. Not for me the "meaningful relationships" the young sophisticates talked about so glibly. Meaningful today, meaningless next Thursday. Not for me the game of musical beds the swingers were playing. I wasn't built that way. I wanted a total commitment. And therein lay the rub. Therein lay the reason my confused mind seesawed back and forth—yes, no, no, yes. If I married Chris there wouldn't *be* a total commitment on his part. And I didn't know if I was big enough and secure enough to live with Chris's dedication to writing. To live with a man who would always be living with the book he was writing, the characters in his mind so alive and demanding of his attention he would have little time for real people—for his wife. Was I willing to play second fiddle to a typewriter—to share him with imaginary people who consumed his time and drained his emotions? Would there be enough left for me? But was there ever enough—for anybody? And I loved the guy. There was no dithering about that. I loved him so much it scared me sometimes. Christopher Patrick Galloway. A big man who for all his size moved lightly on his feet. A big man with a ruggedly handsome face and a squarish, no-nonsense jaw with a cleft in the chin. Thick thatch of chestnut brown hair cut short. Thoughtful, deep-set blue eyes. A quiet, low-keyed guy. A listener, not a talker. A guy who studied human nature and still liked people. A guy who could be gruff, detached, cynical, but who possessed a gentle humor and had poetry in his soul. Christopher Patrick Galloway, my love.

A sharp crackling noise from the fireplace brought me out of my reverie. I sighed. This was no time to ponder the all-

24

important question of whether to marry Chris. In my decrepit state I couldn't think clearly. I put the subject firmly out of mind and picked up Laura's unopened paper from the coffee table. Apathetically I turned pages, glanced at headlines—too heavy-headed to bother reading anything.

Until my eye hit a small-type headline tucked in the bottom corner of page 6: "Woman Found Strangled." I sat up straighter and read on: "Early this morning the body of Kathleen Windsor was found in her apartment at 4900 Winnicott Rd. by a neighbor returning home late. John Gilmour, of the same address, told police he noticed the door of Miss Windsor's apartment was open when he passed it at 2 A.M. and he went to investigate. When there was no answer to his knock, he walked into the apartment and discovered the woman's body on the living room floor. Police officials say the apparent cause of death was strangulation. An autopsy is being performed today. This is the second strangling death on Winnicott Rd. this week. On Monday a woman was found strangled in a garage on Winnicott near Côte St. Luc."

I stared at the black type in stunned disbelief. Then my mind blanked out in a surge of horror. When I fought my way back to awareness, the paper was on the floor. Strangled, my mind whispered, and Strangled! it shouted, as though trying to make itself accept the brutal reality of the word. How awful, how awful! That poor wistful woman with her please-like-me blue eyes. Strangled. And she'd been sitting right on this sofa where I sat now. Instinctively I got up, my legs trembling, and moved to the fireplace.

I huddled close to the leaping flames, like primitive man, who believed that the magic circle of fire protected him from the evil in the darkness beyond. It was ten to seven. Thank God I had asked Chris to come down. I had to talk to somebody. I had doubted Kathleen's story of being followed last night. And I had made fun of her when I'd described her to Laura. A wave of guilt swept over me. But it wouldn't matter to the poor woman now. I had left her safely at home

25

just before eleven last night and three hours later she was dead. But there was no one in the apartment when we took her home—George Matrai had made sure of that. How could it have happened? Someone could have gotten into the building by walking in behind a person with a key, but even if he'd gotten past the doorman, how had he gotten into the apartment? Surely Kathleen, as naïve as she seemed, wouldn't have opened her door to a stranger at that late hour? Especially not after the fright of being followed. And could it possibly be the man who had followed her? But how—?

I jumped when the doorbell rang. It would be Chris, of course. I pressed the buzzer and opened my door—as much as the chain would allow. I wasn't taking any chances. I was frightened, deeply frightened, by the murder of Kathleen Windsor almost on my doorstep. And this on top of the murder last Monday. Both of them just a block away on Winnicott.

It was Chris's face that filled the crack in the door a few moments later. Big, comfortable, comforting Chris, with snow powdering his coat and thick brown hair. He blew a kiss to me with his free hand while I took the chain off. His other hand was encumbered with a big carton and a brown paper bag.

"Tonight we're just good friends, Muffet. I don't want your germs."

"I'm so glad you came tonight, Chris. I've just had the most awful news and I couldn't stand sitting here alone much longer thinking—"

The steady blue eyes regarded me thoughtfully a moment; then Chris set his parcels down on a table and totally forgot his statement about being just good friends for tonight. He enveloped me in a gentle hug, stroking my hair softly with one hand.

"You look frightened to death, Nicky. What's happened to you?" The deep voice was gruff with concern.

26

And suddenly I was pouring it out in disconnected sentences. "In the paper," I babbled, ". . . just five minutes ago I read it in the paper . . . and she was sitting here last night, sitting in the living room, drinking my brandy . . . we took her home, George Matrai and I took her home . . . and everything was all right . . . everything was all right when we left . . . and now she's dead, strangled." I ended in a tone of utter disbelief, feeling the snowy wetness of Chris's coat cold against my feverish face.

He squeezed me gently, then propelled me toward the living room. "I don't know what it's all about, Muffet, but I'll find out in due time. Right now I'm going to give you a stiff drink. That will steady you. Then you can tell me the whole story."

He set one of Laura's big floor cushions by the fireplace and I sank down on it, thinking of Kathleen Windsor. In my mind's eye I saw the anxious, heavy-featured face framed by fat sausage curls, superimposed on a picture of the pristine pink and white bedroom peopled with stuffed animals. Her wistful blue eyes turned into the staring glass-button eyes of a Teddy bear and I shook my head to dissolve the image.

I could hear Chris bustling about in the kitchen. He had been to Laura's apartment often enough to know his way around and often helped me prepare a meal. When he reappeared a few minutes later he was carrying a rum and coke for himself and a snifter glass of brandy for me.

"Brandy's what you need, Muffet. I've put dinner in the oven to keep hot."

He spotted the blanket on the sofa, fetched it and tucked it around my shoulders. "You're shivering. You should be in bed. Wait till you've had a little of your drink before you start talking."

Obediently I drank the brandy in silence, feeling its warmth seep through me, easing the ache in my bones. In a few minutes I felt empty and quiet, drained of emotion. Now,

27

calmly and matter-of-factly, I told Chris about Kathleen Windsor's visit last night. Her story of having been followed. I told him how our janitor and I had taken the woman home and how George Matrai had gone from room to room, checking cupboards, the window leading to the fire escape, even under Kathleen Windsor's bed. Then I got up and retrieved the paper from where it had fallen on the floor in that moment of shock. I handed it to Chris, pointing out the small item on page 6, my eye shrinking from the hideous word "strangled."

The firelight played on his face as he read, throwing a ruddy light on the widely modeled cheekbones, the square, firm jaw with the cleft in the chin. He set the paper down on the floor, looking at me grimly.

"No wonder you're upset, Muffet. Poor unfortunate woman. What a terrible way to die. And it's the second strangling murder on Winnicott this week."

"I feel so guilty about it, Chris. I wondered if I should have reported it to the police, but she didn't want me to and I even doubted her story. I thought she might be imagining she was followed. You know the type—giggles when she's introduced to a man."

"There's no reason to feel guilty. She didn't want you to call the police and it wouldn't have made any difference if you had. A prowl car would have come down, the cops would have made a search around the block and that would have been that. And you can bet the guy wouldn't be hanging around waiting to be picked up. It was probably not the man who followed her at all. How could he have gotten into her apartment? There was no one there when you took her home."

"That's what I can't figure. He could have followed us at a distance when we took Kathleen home and waited until after we'd left. Then walked in behind someone with a key. But how would he know which apartment she was in, unless he knew her by name? And Kathleen would still have had to let him in. Nobody in their right mind would open their door to a stranger at night after being followed."

"If Kathleen was as naïve as you say, he might have bluffed his way in. Possibly he said he was a neighbor with some small household emergency, gambling that Kathleen didn't know all the people on her floor and would just take his word for it. Or it might have been someone she knew. But people you know don't usually strangle you," Chris finished grimly.

"Do you think it could be the same man who murdered the woman in the garage?"

"Two strangling murders on the same street in a week— it looks that way. Sounds like a psychopath on the rampage."

I shuddered and drew the blanket tighter around me and moved closer to the fire. Somewhere, outside in the night, was a strangler prowling the darkened streets looking for another victim?

"Don't think about it any more, Nicky. It's in the hands of the police now. I'm going to get our dinner now and then you're going to bed—where you should have been all day. We'll eat by the fire."

Chris got up and started removing magazines from the coffee table. My head was throbbing again and I went to the bathroom and downed two more aspirin. When I returned, the coffee table was in front of the fire and Chris was putting dishes on it. I was fond of Chinese food and Chris had brought my favorites: beef won ton, lobster, shrimp and scallops on a bed of rice, pineapple chicken and the inevitable chicken chop suey. I contemplated the feast with a weary eye, too sick and upset by the murder to be enthusiastic about anything tonight. Chris, respecting my misery, spoke little during the meal, but I was grateful for his presence on this night of all nights. And true to his word, he didn't stay late. When we finished eating he washed up our dishes and prepared to

29

leave. With his coat and hat on in the hall, Chris surprised me by going back into the living room, opening the drapes and looking at the door that gave onto the lane.

"Looks like a good lock, and you've got a bolt on the door."

I must have looked frightened, because Chris put his arm around me and kissed the top of my head. "You've nothing to worry about," he said gruffly. "Just don't open the door to anybody you don't know." Then, with a few long-legged strides, he was in the hall again.

"Take care of yourself, Nicky. I'll call tomorrow to see how you are."

The door closed behind him and I was left alone with my thoughts. I'd meant to go to bed as soon as Chris left, but now, alone in the apartment without his big, solid presence to sustain me, I felt vaguely uneasy. Reluctant to leave the comforting light and warmth of the fire, I curled up on the sofa again and fell asleep. The shrilling of the phone wakened me and I stubbed my toe against the coffee table rushing to answer it.

"Miss Prescott?" The voice was curt, peremptory.

"She's not home just now. Do you want to leave a message?"

"Where is she?"

It was really none of his business, whoever he was, and I was put off by the arrogant tone. "She is out for the evening," I said coldly. "Do you want to leave a message?"

"Is she out with a boy friend?" the voice demanded brusquely.

"That's really none of your business," I said icily. "If you don't want to leave your name, please hang up."

"I'll call again," the voice snapped, and the receiver banged in my ear.

Well! I thought as I put the receiver down softly. Who could *that* be! Laura wasn't dating anyone as far as I knew and her taste didn't run to arrogant, ill-mannered boors. I

30

glanced at my watch. It was ten-forty. I'd find out soon enough. Laura should be home any time now.

She came in a few minutes later, a surprised look on her face when she saw me sitting in the living room. "I thought you were going to bed early, Nicky?"

"I was—until I read the paper." I picked it up and handed it to her with the warning, "It's going to be a shock, Laura."

She was as shaken by the news as I was and for half an hour we debated the issue—who, how, why—without coming to any definite conclusions. Laura leaned to the theory that the killer was someone Kathleen knew. How else, she said, could he have gotten into her apartment? But then there had been that other murder on Winnicott just five days ago. I wondered if Chris's suggestion was closer to fact. I wondered if a psychopath was on the loose. And if it would have made any difference in the final outcome if I'd notified the police last night that Kathleen Windsor had been followed to our place. And then a thought struck me. Why hadn't it occurred to me before?

"Laura, do you think I should call the police and tell them what happened last night? I don't want to get involved with them if I can help it. Ever since I've been a kid I've been sort of afraid of the police. Do you suppose it could make any difference? I really don't know anything that would be of help. All Kathleen could tell me was that the man was short and wore a dark coat. There must be thousands of short men in Montreal with dark coats."

Laura considered a moment, her piquant face sober. "I can understand your not wanting to get involved and I can't see what good it would do now to tell the police Kathleen had been followed by someone you can't even describe. And frankly, I don't think it *was* the man who followed her—if she *was* followed. No, I wouldn't worry about it, Nicky. If I were you, I'd go to bed and try to forget the whole thing. You look perfectly wretched."

The way I looked couldn't compete with the way I felt and I went to bed, relieved that Laura had backed me up in my reluctance to go to the police. The last thing I wanted to do was get involved with the police.

Chapter 5

Sunday morning I got up feeling like Saturday morning—only more so. It was just past nine when I walked into the kitchen and I didn't expect to find Laura there: she usually slept late on weekends. But there she was in the breakfast nook, sipping coffee and smoking a cigarette.

"What are you doing up in the middle of the night?" I croaked.

"I didn't sleep well and I was awake early this morning. It was probably hearing about that woman's murder last night. That really got to me. How are you this morning? Any better?"

"Better? Yesterday I was one of the walking wounded, today I feel like a stretcher case. I intend to spend the whole day in a horizontal position."

"Poor Nicky. You really have it bad. Are you still shivery?"

"First cousin to Sam McGee from Tennessee. You'll have to *cremate* me before I feel warm again. And speaking of cremation, if you're not expecting any company today, I'll bunk in the living room, where I can be near the fire."

"It's all yours, Nicky. No visitors today. I'll be trying out recipes all afternoon. And tonight I study for school tomorrow."

I popped toast in the toaster and poured myself a large glass of orange juice—for vitamin C. Living with a dietician has made me very nutrition-conscious. My head was pounding again and I disappeared into the bathroom to get aspirin. When I came back Laura had my toast and orange juice on the table and was pouring coffee.

I was almost finished breakfast when I remembered last night's phone call for Laura. I gave her the telephone conversation verbatim and Laura frowned.

"And he asked if I was out with my boy friend? I can't imagine who it could be. Whoever he is, I don't like the sound of him."

A minute later Laura set down her coffee cup, lips compressed in a tight line of annoyance. "I think I know now . . . arrogant, impertinent . . . in fact I'm sure—Norman Roxburgh. It sounds just like him!"

I'd never heard the name before. "Who's Norman Roxburgh?" I rasped.

"A man in my restaurant administration class. We went out for coffee a couple of times after school and the second time was enough for me. He came all over possessive and domineering—acted as though he *owned* me—after buying me two cups of coffee! Wanted to go into business with me —practically tried to force a deal down my throat. He's been hounding me to go out with him for weeks. Thursday night I thought I'd fixed him, told him I had two steady boy friends and couldn't possibly find time for any more." Laura sighed. "And now he's going to start bugging me at home. If he calls again, say I'm out—whether I am or not—and hang up before he can go into his third-degree routine." Laura got up and stretched her supple frame. "You go and sleep. I'll get a good fire started in the living room for you."

I dressed again in my corduroys and cable-knit sweater and wearily took my aching body to the living room, along with a blanket and a box of Kleenex. Laura was putting wood on the fire.

33

"Do you want me to waken you if you're asleep when Chris calls?"

"No, let me sleep. Tell him I'll call him later in the day."

I lay shivering on the sofa—thinking of Kathleen Windsor. Laura and I had avoided talking about the murder this morning, but as soon as I relaxed and let go, the subject filled my mind to the exclusion of everything else. Resolutely I made my mind go blank and drifted closer to the shore of the Kingdom of Sleep. At the shore checkpoint, a woman with earnest blue eyes timidly asked for my papers. When I presented them, the huge plush paw of a Teddy bear took them angrily and tore them up—glaring at me from glass-button eyes. I woke sneezing violently and reached for the Kleenex beside me.

Laura popped her head around the corner of the door. "Since you're awake, Nicky, how about some lunch? It's after one."

"Already? I just got to sleep. I haven't the strength to get up."

"Stay where you are, I'll bring it in."

"Something light," I called after Laura's vanishing head. "I'm not really hungry."

She was back a few minutes later with a bowl of tomato soup and crackers, a strawberry custard and a large glass of orange juice—more vitamin C, no doubt. I ate from the coffee table in front of the sofa, while Laura hovered about like Florence Nightingale.

"Chris called to see how you were. He said to take care of yourself and not to worry; you still look like Cleopatra to him—even with a cold in the head. And he said not to bother phoning if you don't feel like talking. He'll call you tomorrow."

I finished my lunch and went to sleep, cheered by the thought that I still looked like Cleopatra to Chris. Love *is* blind, I thought, with a rush of happiness that did more than fires and blankets to warm my shivery body.

34

It seemed to me I'd just gotten to sleep again when Laura was gently shaking me awake.

"Sorry to waken you, Nicky, but I'm afraid you're going to have company."

"Company?" I croaked. "In this condition? Who is it, Laura?"

"Your Aunt Emily. I knew you didn't feel up to seeing anyone and I tried to put her off, but when the dear heard you were sick, she insisted she must come and see for herself how you were. She said she'd only stay a few minutes."

I groaned and sat up. Laura grinned in sympathy with me. "I'll give her a cup of tea after she's been here half an hour, Nicky. Aunt Emily always leaves as soon as she's had her tea."

I sneezed vehemently after Laura's retreating back. It isn't that I'm not fond of Aunt Emily. I wouldn't trade her for a dozen of anybody else's aunts. She's a blithe spirit, a spring breeze, a tonic—but she requires a certain amount of energy to keep up with. Since I am twenty-four and Aunt Emily sixty-two, this shouldn't be a problem, but in my wretched state I knew that just looking at her would exhaust me.

It has been variously suggested to me that Aunt Emily has a slate loose, is off her rocker, has lost some of her marbles, is not all there—and other euphemisms for the word "crazy." All these judgments of Emily Teasdale are unjust. The truth of the matter is that she's eccentric; in other words, she's gloriously herself. Mind you, herself changes with dizzying rapidity these days and it may be that Aunt Emily is suffering an identity crisis rather late in life. In just the last six months, for example, she's been into Zen Buddhism, Yoga and Krishna Consciousness. But if Aunt Emily is trying to find herself, she's having an awful lot of fun doing it. Just recently she's been attending Sunday feasts at the Park Avenue Hare Krishna Temple. Many a Sunday she's dropped in, with tilaks painted on her forehead, one hundred and eight japa prayer beads adorning her scrawny neck, to report

35

on the proceedings in glowing terms. She loves the food, the incense, the dancing and clapping. And as Aunt Emily puts it, "You really get good vibes dancing past the Jagannatha deities." If this seems inconsistent with attendance at St. Simon's Church, Aunt Emily blinks it. Her inconsistency is part of her charm. I take my aunt in stride now, although I admit I was a bit shaken up the day last summer when she dropped in and invited me outside "to see something," smiling beatifically all the while. The "something" proved to be a big, sporty-looking red motorcycle.

"Had her first run today," Aunt Emily told me, beaming, before I could say anything appropriate. "Handles like a trouper and she tops out at seventy-five miles per hour with no trouble, even though she's only got four gears in the transmission. Starts on the first kick and keeps moving right along. Rough terrain doesn't faze her; she hugs the road like a lover—"

I looked at her with awe. "You mean that thing is *yours* . . . you *rode* it over here?"

"That's what I've been trying to tell you, dear. Want to go for a ride?"

I hastily declined and Aunt Emily looked disappointed. Then she straddled the beast, gave something a good kick and vrooomed off, small in the saddle, while I gaped openmouthed after her.

For months I'd expected her to come to disaster momentarily, but not Emily Teasdale. She did admit though that riding her noisy red charger would be a little tricky on snow and ice and had promised to put it away for the winter, much to my relief.

Simultaneously I sneezed and the doorbell buzzed. Laura went to answer it and a minute later the object of my reflections was in front of me. Aunt Emily looks like a bird about to take wing any second. As spare and finely boned as a bird, with a small, pointed face and bird-bright black eyes that traveled with nervous quickness from object to ob-

36

ject as though on the alert for danger. The shining eyes consumed my face while she unbuttoned a long black cape to reveal knickered knees and diamond-checked knee socks. I tried to put enthusiasm into my voice.

"Hello, Aunt Emily, it was nice of you to drop in."

"You sound like a frog, dear, but never mind, they turn into princes, you know," she consoled me.

Sometimes there is an Alice in Wonderland quality about my aunt's conversations. I've grown accustomed to it now and when I can't think of a suitable rejoinder to some of her odd remarks, I remain comfortably silent, with no sense of strain.

She now had her hand on my head. "Feels feverish," she clucked to Laura, hopping on one foot. "See that she gets lots of fluid and rest. You're not going to work tomorrow, are you, dear?"

"No, Aunt Emily, I'm staying put until I feel like a human being again."

"Only sensible thing to do. I'm so sorry you're sick, dear. But you'll feel better in a few days. Laura, do you suppose I could have a wee drink—maybe wine. Had terrible news today at church. Made myself a good cup of tea when I got home, but it didn't help a mite. I'm all unstrung."

"Of course, Aunt Emily. Take your cape off and sit down."

Laura went for the drink while Aunt Emily doffed her cape and perched on the sofa beside me, tucking the blanket around my shoulders. "Have to keep warm, dear," she said distractedly, her small, sharp nose quivering. "I hope it won't upset you, Nicky, when you're ill, but I really have to talk about it. I'll wait till Laura comes in so she can hear it too. I never dreamed—"

Laura returned just then with a glass of sherry and gave it to Aunt Emily. She took a few quick mouthfuls, lifting her gray head after every sip to peer nervously around her. Laura squatted cross-legged on the floor in front of us.

"What's happened, Aunt Emily?"

"Murder," she said dramatically. "Cold-blooded murder right in the choir. The second one this week."

I knew Aunt Emily sang in the choir at St. Simon's Church. It hadn't occurred to me that Kathleen Windsor had attended the same church. "What was her name?" I asked, knowing the answer already.

"Kathleen Windsor. Lived near us, Nicky, on Winnicott."

"And the other woman that was murdered this week was in your choir, too?"

"That's right. Terrible shock to everybody. Elsie murdered on Monday and Kathleen on Friday. And both of them living on Winnicott. Everybody in the choir warning me to be careful. It does make a body nervous, but no one would bother killing an old woman like me." Aunt Emily took another drink from her glass and shook her head in disbelief. "It's so hard to believe. I was talking to Kathleen after choir practice Friday and a few hours later she was murdered."

Laura and I started talking at the same time; then I stopped and let Laura tell the story of Kathleen Windsor's visit to our apartment the night she was killed.

Aunt Emily's bright eyes were liquid with sympathy when Laura finished her account. "Poor woman, what a dreadful way to die. And she seemed so happy when she left choir practice. We usually have our practices on Wednesday and Sunday, but Mrs. Anderson called a special practice for Friday night because we were singing folk music for the service today.

"In fact, Kathleen seemed happy ever since her mother went into the hospital two months ago. I guess it was the first time in her life she was ever away from her mother. The mother had a real strangle hold on her. Girl had no life of her own. Choir practice Wednesday, church and practice on Sunday, Sunday afternoon at her Aunt Louise's—and had to account for any other time she was out of the apartment. And she could have had such a wonderful life . . . had an independent income of fifteen thousand dollars a

38

year from her father. He made his money in mining . . . left the mother pretty early in the game and tried to get custody of the daughter, but the mother fought it through the courts and won. By the time Kathleen was of age she couldn't have broken away from her mother to save her life. Well, at least the last few months of her life were happy. Must have felt to Kathleen like being let out of prison. Stayed late talking to me after choir practice Friday. Normally she'd scurry off home the minute practice was over."

Aunt Emily drained the last of her sherry and cocked her head as though listening for something. She had once told me that if you sat very still and listened with your soul, you could get vibrations from outer space. And Aunt Emily was sitting very still, seemingly unaware that anybody was in the room with her. We waited until she came back to us.

The frail neck suddenly tilted upright again; intelligence returned to the shining black eyes. "You know, girls, I don't know what to make of it, but I was getting strange vibes from Kathleen the last while. I said she was happier and she was—face all lit up at church—but at the same time she seemed more nervous than usual—did an awful lot of giggling. And one Sunday she didn't stay for the practice after service—said her aunt wasn't well and she was going to visit her early. I didn't stay for practice that Sunday either —had a cold and wasn't much good for singing. Left just after Kathleen and here I see her getting into a car with a man a block from the church. Probably a friend of the family who just happened to be passing by. Still it seemed a bit odd—"

The idea of Kathleen Windsor having secret trysts was just too fantastic to consider. "Do you think it was a boy friend, Aunt Emily?"

"Gracious, no! Kathleen was afraid of men. But there was just something about her that was different the last few months—"

"You said yourself, Aunt Emily, she was happy being out

from under her mother's thumb. At the same time, she was probably nervous about being on her own for the first time in her life."

"That makes sense, Nicky. Anyway, talking about the poor soul won't bring her back. I'm going to go now, dear, and let you rest."

Aunt Emily bounced up suddenly, hopped to a clear space in the middle of the floor, pirouetted on one foot and sang in a clear, strong soprano: "He wore flowing robes and sandals and he came with love for all . . ."

She stopped as suddenly as she'd begun. "We sang it at the folk service today," she enlightened me. Without waiting for a comment, Aunt Emily seized her cape, donned it with great furling gestures and skipped toward the hall. She gave me a last admonition as she pulled on her boots. "Remember dear, lots of sleep and fluids. I'll call tomorrow and see how you are. 'Bye, girls."

As I opened the door to let my aunt out, my eyes traveled across the hall. The door of Sybil Hepworth's apartment was open just a crack. Closing the door firmly on my nosy neighbor's spying, I returned to the living room with Laura.

My apartmentmate suggested a drink and forthwith produced same—a hot rum for me, a daiquiri for herself. While we sipped our drinks, we mulled over the information my aunt had given us about Kathleen Windsor. But we didn't pursue the subject long. People usually relish talking about murders, but this one was a little too close to home for comfort.

Laura commented that Aunt Emily wasn't in her usual form today. We'd had only one snatch of song and no dancing at all.

"And she didn't shut out the world of maya once," I added.

Laura's pixie face looked puzzled. "What might the world of maya be?" she asked.

"The world outside—a world that holds us in its octopus

40

tentacles of materialism—a world of illusion, according to Krishna followers. When Aunt Emily sits Buddha-fashion on the floor and squeezes her eyes tight shut, she's shutting out the world of maya."

Laura looked intrigued. "Is *that* what she's doing? With Aunt Emily one never knows!" She shook her long red mane and uncurled herself from her chair. "I must get back to my baking. You go back to your interrupted sleep. I'll waken you for supper."

The rest of the day went by in a feverish haze. I drowsed until suppertime, feeling even in sleep the sharp stabs in my bones.

Laura brought supper to me in the living room, asking for my comments on a new German torte she had baked—a sponge cake and marmalade confection, frosted with vanilla icing and chopped nuts and topped with glazed strawberries. A cold does nothing to sharpen one's taste buds, but I could still recognize a winner when I tasted one, and told Laura so.

I slept again after supper and woke to find Laura studying at her desk by the living room windows. She told me that Norman Roxburgh had called her while I was asleep and had been quite obnoxious—trying to *bully* her into going out with him. I said goodnight to Laura at ten o'clock, soaked in a hot bath for half an hour, took some aspirin and went to bed, setting my clock for eight-thirty. I wasn't going to work in the morning, but I'd have to call the principal of Kensington School for Girls and let her know.

Chapter 6

I sneezed myself awake on Monday just before my alarm was due to go off. My head throbbed dully, but I made one encouraging discovery when I got up: the sharp, needlelike pains in my bones were less intense. I supposed the gremlins were getting tired of stabbing me. I splashed cold water on my face to waken myself; then I called Miss Eden at school to tell her I wouldn't be in. She offered her condolences and told me not to come back until I was well. That taken care of, I had a light breakfast. Laura had left for work, but the coffee was still hot. After breakfast, I went through the ritual of lighting the fire in the living room, bringing a blanket and Kleenex in from the bedroom and curling up on the sofa again.

I lay thinking with dismay of all I had to do before I left for Jamaica on the eleventh of December. I'd been buying my Christmas presents one at a time for the past two months and everyone getting a gift was now accounted for, but I still had to wrap them all and distribute them. And I'd intended to make a dress for my vacation the weekend just past. To save the money for the long vacations I've been taking in Europe the last couple of years, I have to cut corners every way possible, and I've found I can save more than 50 per cent of the cost of my clothes by making them myself. I had pretty well everything I needed for a vacation in the sun, but I wanted to make one smashing evening dress and I'd found a gorgeous peony-pink flowered chiffon on sale at Marshall's one Thursday night and I knew I had to have it. I could just see it made up—a halter-topped, voluminous-skirted romance of a dress. Well, I still had another weekend left to make it on, but I was certainly going to be busy.

The crackling of the fire lulled me and I fell asleep dreaming of sapphire blue waters lapping a palm-fringed shore. I slept in fits and starts the rest of the morning. After lunch I went out to the lobby to see if there was any mail in our box. I was just about to close the mailbox when the door of T. Oliphant's apartment opened and he emerged, carrying a brown carton with string. The stooped, cadaverous figure swerved to the left as he approached me—as if to put as much space between us as possible. As he passed me, his thick-lensed eyes glittered at me a second; then they slid to the region of my knees and his mouth knit up in a tight pucker. I felt a sudden chill go through me. The look on his face—just the way he'd looked at Kathleen Windsor last Friday night when we'd passed him on our way out. And his eyes then had seemed to focus on her knees. A sudden thought hit me: Was it the *pants* he was staring at? Kathleen Windsor had been wearing pants under her knee-length coat and I was wearing pants today. Did Mr. Oliphant, by chance, object to women in trousers? Did it smack too much of Women's Lib to this strange gaunt man with the ghastly pallor?

I hurried back to the apartment and the compelling magnet of the fire—somehow so reassuring and comforting. The last thought in my mind before I went to sleep again concerned our odd neighbor. I couldn't go along with Sybil Hepworth's wild theory that he was making bombs, but I concurred wholeheartedly with Laura's opinion that T. Oliphant was a woman hater.

I slept most of the afternoon away and ate a lonely supper of chicken pie and baked apple by the warmth of the fire. Laura ate downtown on Monday night. She had to be at school at seven-thirty and coming home for dinner first would make it a hectic scramble to get out on time. Although, on Thursday, her other school night, she did come home and make the hectic scramble in the interests of economy.

Aunt Emily phoned about eight to find out how I was, and Chris called a few minutes later with the same purpose. Chris also asked if I thought I'd be in shape Friday to see a comedy with Guy and Lisa Sabourin. Lisa was a friend of mine from school days. She'd married Guy Sabourin eight months ago and the four of us went out together frequently. Neither Chris nor I was too enthusiastic about Guy, but we both loved Lisa. Chris told me the evening was the Sabourins' treat and we'd have a buffet supper after the show at their place. I told Chris to accept on our behalf: if I wasn't better by Friday I never would be.

After our phone call, I turned on the TV and listlessly dialed from channel to channel till I hit one featuring an old movie. I propped myself up with pillows and watched it from the sofa. Laura came in so quietly I didn't hear her and I started when she materialized beside me.

"I just wanted to see if you were decent, Nicky. I'm bringing someone in." Her voice was strangely tight and whispery.

I sat up quickly and folded my blanket, not wanting to be caught looking like a neurasthenic. Laura had already retreated to the hall and a few moments later she was back with a tall, slim stranger. Laura introduced him as Julian Brooks and after the introductions were over and everybody was seated I noticed that not only did Laura's voice sound funny—she didn't look right either. She was as pale as death and her eyes were stary. I looked harder and saw that the pupils were dilated. Before I could ask what was wrong, the man who had brought Laura home spoke. I detected a slight accent in his voice—a well-bred English accent.

"Miss Prescott has had a shaking up, Miss Nugent. Do you have anything to drink? Brandy or—"

I was on my feet before he finished speaking. I *knew* something was wrong and although I was burning with curi-

44

osity, the questions could keep until Laura had had something to fortify her. As I poured brandy in the kitchen, my heart gave a sudden, unexpected thump of fear. On Friday night I had poured brandy for Kathleen Windsor.

When I gave Laura the drink I noticed that her hand was slightly unsteady, but she gave me a ghost of a smile. I intended to hold the questions until she'd drunk enough of the brandy to steady her, but Laura turned to Julian Brooks and said in her whispery voice:

"Will you tell her, Julian? I don't want to talk about it yet."

The stranger turned his concerned glance from Laura to me. He'd be about thirty-six, I thought, with thin, sensitive features and dark blond hair that just brushed the collar of his expensively tailored suit. While Laura slowly sipped the brandy, Julian Brooks gave me the story.

He had been driving along Côte St. Luc a block west of Winnicott when he'd seen, in the distance ahead of him, a woman struggling on the sidewalk with a man. The man appeared to be trying to drag the woman into the park that covered the entire block between Winnicott and Godfrey Street on the north side of Côte St. Luc. Julian had speeded up his car until he reached the spot where he'd seen the couple. By that time they had vanished into the park. A scream from Laura had given him direction and he'd plunged into the park after them, with a shout of warning to the attacker. Julian had burst through a screen of trees into a small clearing in time to see the man fleeing into the deeper darkness of the forestlike park, while Laura cowered on her knees, shaking with fear. Julian, after a brief word of reassurance to Laura, had rushed into the darkness after the assailant but had failed to find him. Then he'd returned to Laura and driven her home.

As I listened to Julian Brooks's account of what had happened, a series of conflicting emotions shook me. First, horror, horror at what might have happened to Laura; then fear, a deep, all-pervading fear. Just a week ago a woman had been dragged off the street into a garage on Winnicott and strangled; last Friday Kathleen Windsor had rushed to our apartment with a story of being followed. A few hours later she was dead of strangulation. Was a psychopath roaming the streets, as Chris had suggested? But overriding the horror and fear was a surge of gratitude toward this man who had bravely rushed into the darkness after an assailant—not knowing whether the man was armed or not.

"It was wonderful of him, wasn't it, Nicky?"

Laura's voice was normal now and the color had returned to her face. She looked at Julian Brooks with gratitude and admiration in her eyes and the subject of her adoration flushed and stammered:

"I say, Laura, what else could a man *do* in the circumstances? I only wish I'd caught the rotter."

"Did he hurt you, Laura?" I asked anxiously.

"I'll probably find a few bruises on my arms tomorrow but nothing more serious."

"You're feeling better now, are you, Laura?" Julian Brooks's tone was solicitous.

"Yes, I'm all right now, thanks."

He took a gold cigarette case from his coat pocket and extended it to Laura and me. I don't smoke, but Laura and Julian took cigarettes and he lit them with a gold cigarette lighter.

"I think," said Julian, "we'd better call the police about this."

Laura and I were both in agreement, so I showed Julian out to the phone in the hall and let him place the call.

While he was talking to the police Laura and I decided between us not to mention the incident of Kathleen Windsor being followed to our home. We should have reported it before and now we both felt a little guilty in the light of events that followed. To be truthful, we were afraid the police might be annoyed with us.

46

Julian returned to the living room with information that the police would be down in ten minutes. I treated him to some of Laura's rye and we made small talk until the door buzzer signaled the arrival of the police.

A few minutes later Constable Yvon Paquette and Sergeant Claude Montcalm were sitting in our living room. Constable Paquette, the silent partner, had a notebook and pencil at the ready. Sergeant Montcalm, big, crew-cut and competent-looking, asked the questions while Constable Paquette's nimble pencil raced across the page.

Again it was Julian who recounted the details of the attack, but some questions had to be put to Laura. What did the man look like? Had she ever seen him before? Where did she first see him? Where was she coming from? Etc. etc. Laura did the best she could, but I could see that talking about it upset her and she looked relieved when the spate of questions ended and Constable Paquette closed his notebook.

"You were very lucky M. Brooks happened along when he did, Mlle. Prescott." Sergeant Montcalm's voice was quiet and his eyes were deadly serious. I wondered if he was thinking of the two strangling deaths. "We're having this area watched right now and we'll put an extra man on the park. A dangerous spot."

"Is there any chance of getting him, Sergeant?" asked Julian.

Sergeant Montcalm bunched one hand into a fist and punched his other hand. "If he keeps operating in this area, we'll get him," he promised grimly.

I knew then that Sergeant Montcalm *was* thinking of the two strangling murders. The full impact of what might have happened to Laura tonight struck me like a blow and I gave a convulsive shudder.

Sergeant Montcalm gave me a long look from hard blue eyes. He got up slowly and Constable Paquette followed his lead. "If you ever see anyone who resembles the man who attacked you, notify us at once. And be careful. Don't walk

47

on the park side of the street. Keep in well-lighted areas and don't come home late at night alone." With this frightening advice, the two policemen took their departure.

I felt the need of a drink myself now and Laura and Julian looked like they could use another, so I made drinks for all three of us: rye for Julian and me and another brandy for Laura. It was then that Laura brought up Kathleen Windsor and speculated whether the man who had followed Kathleen could have been the same man who had attacked her. Julian looked puzzled, of course, so Laura told him the whole story of Kathleen Windsor's visit to our apartment the night she was murdered. He was startled to learn there had been a murder only a block away from us and wondered if the police thought Laura's attacker could have been the man who killed Kathleen Windsor.

Laura explained to Julian that we hadn't reported the incident of Kathleen Windsor's visit to us when we learned of her murder because we had no information that would be of help to the police and that tonight we hadn't mentioned it because we were a little afraid they might be annoyed with us for not informing them sooner. But, as Laura said, telling the police now that the woman had been followed last Friday wasn't going to do the least bit of good. And in any case, we weren't even sure the woman *had* been followed; she might have been imagining it.

I don't think Julian was quite convinced that we'd done the right thing, but he agreed that we had no information that would be of assistance to the police in their search for Kathleen Windsor's murderer. And he agreed with Laura that the man who had killed Kathleen Windsor was probably someone she knew. How else explain how he got into the apartment? Julian suggested that maybe it was a jealous boy friend, but Laura and I scoffed at this.

"If you'd seen her and talked to her for five minutes, Mr. Brooks," I said, "you'd know she couldn't have a boy friend. No man would be attracted to her. She was like a child. My

48

aunt *did* see her getting into a car with a man after church one Sunday and she thought it a bit odd. I asked her if she thought it could be Kathleen's boy friend, but my aunt scotched that idea. She said Kathleen Windsor was *afraid* of men. And my aunt knew her pretty well. They both sang in St. Simon's choir. Aunt Emily was talking to her at choir practice a few hours before she was murdered."

"Well, I guess a jealous boy friend is out then. Whoever did it, I hope they catch the rotter soon, Miss Nugent."

"My friends call me Nicky."

Julian blushed boyishly. "Well, then, Nicky it is, and I'm Julian."

We talked another half-hour or so; then Julian took his leave, earnestly exhorting us to be careful when we were out at night alone.

During the course of our conversation, we'd learned that he was a free-lance furniture designer who hoped to buy a furniture plant and manufacture and market his own designs soon and that he lived in plush Somerset Place, an apartment-hotel for executives in Westmount. I'd also learned that he was interested in Laura Prescott, if the admiring glances he'd been giving her were any indication. And if I wasn't mistaken, Laura was interested in Julian Brooks. Or maybe she was just grateful, which would be understandable. At any rate, she commented that he seemed very nice and if it hadn't been for him . . . She left the sentence unfinished, and that was understandable, too. Laura could remain composed under the most rattling circumstances and on the surface she was calm now, but I knew she had been deeply shaken by the night's experience and didn't want to talk about it.

I suggested that she take a sleeping pill to make sure she got some sleep and she agreed that it was a good idea. Otherwise. she said, she'd be having nightmares all night. We said goodnight at the bathroom door and I gave her an extra-generous smile. I was pretty fond of Laura—and tonight I might have lost her.

Chapter 7

On Tuesday I got up early, in a more cheerful frame of mind. I felt up to going back to work, but knowing how Miss Eden was about people *spreading germs,* I decided to wait another day. My cheerfulness was subdued somewhat when Laura pulled up the sleeve of her sweater at the breakfast table and displayed a badly bruised arm. Then the events of last night came flooding back and again I felt the unpleasant sensation of fear.

"He certainly wasn't gentle, Laura."

"You're right there, Nicky. He had his hands gripped around my arm in a vise of steel. Dragged me right off my feet in the park. It was just then Julian shouted, and he let go of me and ran. I hope the police get him; I'm going to be frightened every time I come home along Côte St. Luc. At least now I'll know enough to walk on the south side rather than the park side of the street."

"Sergeant Montcalm said they'd put a man on the park, and that will probably scare him away pretty fast." I said this with great conviction to allay Laura's fears, but inwardly I was frightened. I was going to be very careful coming home alone at nights myself.

After Laura had left for work, I washed some lingerie, made up the fire in the living room and spent most of the day, with a break for lunch, on the sofa. In the afternoon I leafed through some of Laura's home-decorating magazines—looking for ideas for my own future home. At six o'clock I got up and fixed dinner for Laura and myself. We were on our dessert when the door buzzer pealed. Laura went to answer it. I heard voices in the living room and then Laura came into the kitchen, looking a little frightened.

"A detective lieutenant from Homicide, Nicky. He wants to talk to you."

I jumped up guiltily. What could he want of me? Did they know about Kathleen Windsor's visit . . . ? But how . . . ?

Laura fell into step behind me as I headed for the living room. "I'll give you moral support," she whispered.

The man who rose to greet me when I entered the living room was of medium height, with a weary face and bleak gray eyes that looked as though they'd seen too much of the seamy side of life.

"Lieutenant Noël Philippe," he introduced himself, in a slightly Gallic voice. "I have a few questions to ask about Kathleen Windsor."

"Kathleen Windsor?" I stammered, feeling the telltale flush of guilt suffuse my face. Oh God, why hadn't I said something to Sergeant Montcalm when he was here last night?

"Kathleen Windsor," he repeated softly, the bitter gray eyes boring into my skull. "You were the last person to see her alive—you and George Matrai."

He knew all about it. But how? I made an attempt to regain my poise—not to be intimidated by the pale, tired face and cynical eyes. "I don't know if we were the last persons to see her alive. We did take her home on Friday night. But how did you know?"

"Miss Windsor's picture was in today's paper. We got an anonymous phone call that you and the janitor of this building were seen leaving here with her about a quarter to eleven on Friday night." The lieutenant smiled a wry, one-sided smile. "Were you aware that the woman had been murdered, mademoiselle?"

To my annoyance, I found myself flushing again. "Yes, I saw it in Saturday night's paper." My voice sounded weak.

Lieutenant Philippe raised a bushy eyebrow. "But you

didn't think it of importance to tell the police you saw the woman an hour before she was murdered? Or that she was followed that night?"

I was on the defensive now. "I offered to call the police for her, but she didn't want me to. And when I read about the murder in the paper I didn't think the information I had would be of any help. She couldn't even describe the man clearly."

Lieutenant Philippe nodded thoughtfully; then he turned to Laura. "And I have a report, mademoiselle, that last night you were followed and attacked on your way home. The police were right here, but you still didn't think they would be interested in knowing that a woman had come to your home only a few days ago after being followed—a woman who was murdered the same night?"

Putting it the way the detective was putting it, our position seemed indefensible. "I'm sorry, Lieutenant Philippe, I guess I should have reported it, but at the time it didn't seem—"

He gave a Gallic shrug. "Mademoiselle, things that don't seem important at the time often are. And no doubt," he added, "you did not wish to become involved with the police." There was a reproachful note in his quiet voice. He was looking straight through me with those disillusioned gray eyes of his and I flushed.

"I guess you're right, Lieutenant. Police have always sort of scared me."

He sighed. "That is the trouble, mademoiselle; we are all afraid of the police because we are all guilty. But we cannot perform miracles. We cannot apprehend killers when the public will not co-operate with us." He took a small notebook and pen from his coat pocket. "I have already talked to George Matrai, but I want your account of Friday night. If you will give me, please, the story of Miss Windsor coming here last Friday. Do not omit anything, no matter how trivial —remember, what doesn't seem important at the time often is."

I gave Lieutenant Philippe the story of my encounter with Kathleen Windsor, trying to remember it in the smallest detail. The detective interrupted occasionally to ask a question, but most of the time he was busy jotting down what I said. When I'd finished my story the lieutenant sighed wearily and put his book away.

"It is not enough there is one murder in the area. There must be two."

"Do you think the two murders are related?" I asked.

"Who can say, mademoiselle? A psychopath reads of the affair in the paper and his feverish brain is inspired to duplicate the act. Thus, one murder often leads to another. The main similarity in the two cases is the method of murder—but there is an important difference. The Windsor woman had been sexually molested. The Grunberger woman had not. Although there is a possibility that the Grunberger killer may have intended to molest his victim but did not have the time. The car was running in the garage and he knew the owner might return at any moment. We may be dealing with a sexual deviate. There is sometimes a sexual element in strangling murders."

I shuddered to think what poor childish Kathleen Windsor might have endured before she died and thanked God again for the timely presence of Julian Brooks last night when Laura was attacked on her way home from school.

Lieutenant Philippe got up slowly, as though reluctant to leave the comfort of his cushioned chair. The bags under his eyes, coupled with the sad, weary expression—which seemed permanent—gave him the look of a tired bloodhound. But the bitter eyes were keen as he said goodbye to us at the door.

"If you should recall anything later that you did not think of tonight, you will, of course, call me, mademoiselle?" It was an order, not a question.

As I closed the door on the detective, I saw the door of Sybil Hepworth's apartment silently closing. Then I remembered that she had been at her door when George Matrai and I had left the building with Kathleen Windsor last Friday. So Sybil Hepworth was the anonymous caller who had led the police to our door. I should have known.

We returned to our interrupted dinner in a subdued and thoughtful mood. Both of us were upset by Lieutenant Philippe's visit and the talk of Kathleen Windsor's murder. And both of us knew, though neither of us voiced the thought, that the man who had dragged Laura into the park last night might well have been the murderer of Kathleen Windsor and Elsie Grunberger.

By unspoken agreement neither of us discussed the topic of Lieutenant Philippe's visit. I merely remarked that it was Sybil Hepworth who had called the police about George Matrai and me, and Laura commented dryly that the news didn't come as too much of a surprise.

After dinner I watched TV while Laura studied at her desk in the living room. At eight-thirty the phone rang and Laura went to answer it. She came back with a slightly flushed face and a bounce in her step I hadn't noticed before. But her voice, when she spoke, was carefully casual.

"That was Julian Brooks. He wanted to know how I was today."

"How did he get your phone number?" I asked, surprised.

"He got it from our phone when he called the police last night. He's a pleasant change from some of the aggressive types operating around town these days. Some of them come on like gangbusters." There was a slightly bitter note in Laura's voice when she made this last remark and I wondered if she was thinking of Norman Roxburgh—or of someone else.

"He asked me if I'd like to go out to dinner with him Friday. He asked in such a nice way. Said he was awfully taken with me and awfully sorry about what happened last night and he hoped I wouldn't think him too presumptuous but he wondered if—"

"I hope you said yes," I interrupted eagerly, thinking it

54

was time Laura got back into circulation again and that Julian Brooks had seemed the type of man any girl would be glad to circulate with.

Laura grinned her gamin grin and her freckles danced across the bridge of her nose. "You're just dying to see me in tandem, aren't you?" Then the pert face turned serious. "Of course I said yes; I couldn't turn him down after what he did for me last night and I *did* rather like him. I'm looking forward to it."

I was about to ask where they were going for dinner when the phone pealed again. This time I answered it. It was Aunt Emily.

"Hello, dear," she piped, "are you feeling better now?"

"Much, Aunt Emily. I'm going back to work tomorrow. How are you?"

"Fine. Just fine. Glad you're better, dear. I'm busy, busy. Seems to take so much time getting from place to place on the bus. I'll be glad when winter's over and I can get my motorbike on the road again. I just tooled around the city last year, but next summer I'm going to try her out on a run or two to the boondocks.

"Now, what I wanted to know, Nicky: Would Laura do me a big favor and bake a birthday cake for Donald? I'd pay for the ingredients of course. Laura makes such beautiful cakes. I couldn't buy one half as good and it *is* a special occasion. Donald's such a nice boy—so much *soul!*"

"I'll ask her, Aunt Emily, but she might like to know who Donald is."

"Donald Hammill—I got him from the drop-in center."

"The drop-in center?"

"The drop-in center for homeless youth on Bleury. He comes from Windsor. Couldn't stand it at home and ran away. Says he won't go back again, no matter what. I took him home with me on Monday. The boy needs a home. Intend to keep him until he can find a job and look after himself."

Nothing Aunt Emily does surprises me, but I couldn't

help but wonder what she was doing at a drop-in center for homeless youth. But then, Aunt Emily pretty well covers the waterfront. And her birdlike body houses a giving heart. She feeds squirrels, birds and horses from an enormous handbag stocked with nuts, bread crumbs and apples. And she's forever taking in stray cats and dogs and—on occasion—people. Her charity toward animals was to be applauded, but I worried about her picking up people so casually. It was one way to get into trouble.

"It's good of you to take him," I said doubtfully, "but are you sure he's all right, Aunt Emily? I mean, you don't know anything about him—"

"Don't worry, Nicky, Donald's a good boy. Although I'm a little afraid he's flirting with Mary Jane, and Tony's going steady with her."

I took the hurdles one at a time. "Who's Mary Jane and what's wrong with flirting with her? Has she got leprosy or something?"

"Marijuana, dear. Mary Jane is marijuana," said my aunt patiently.

Every girl needs an Aunt Emily to set her straight. "Oh, I see. And who's Tony?"

"Tony Bartha," explained my aunt in her thin treble. "He was with Donald at the drop-in center and he didn't have anywhere to go, so I took him home, too. But I don't much care for him. He acts sort of funny and I may not keep him long. But to get back to the cake, dear, I just found out tonight it's Donald's birthday on Friday and I hope it's not too short notice for Laura."

I didn't like the sound of Tony Bartha, but I didn't say anything. I told Aunt Emily I'd ask Laura about the cake and left the phone with the uneasy feeling that my aunt might have bitten off more than she could chew. A minute later I reported back that Laura would be happy to bake an extraspecial cake for Donald and it would be ready Wednesday night. My aunt was profuse in her thanks to Laura and told

56

me to be sure Laura kept track of the cost of making it. And Aunt Emily would be out Wednesday and Thursday. Would it be all right if she picked the cake up Friday? I saw no reason why not. Both Laura and I would be going out that night, but I wouldn't be leaving before seven. It was agreed she would come by for the cake around six on Friday and we said goodbye, Aunt Emily advising me to dress warmly when I went back to work tomorrow and get lots of sleep until my cold was completely better. I couldn't really say why I hadn't told my aunt about the attack on Laura the night before. Somehow I just didn't want to talk about it.

There was one more phone call that night—from Norman Roxburgh, badgering her to go out with him. Laura was practically livid with anger. "For sheer persistence, Nicky, I've never met anyone like him. I'll have to hit him with a sledge hammer before he understands that I don't like him. I told him if he called again, I'd get an unlisted phone number. And Thursday at school I'm going to see if I can get transferred into the other class in restaurant administration. There are two, fortunately. I can't stand the *sight* of that man now!"

Chapter 8

It was good to get out of the apartment and back to work on Wednesday, even though my "in" basket was piled high with material to be dealt with one way or another. I'd felt like a caged lion the last two days at home. I went to work with a will on the mountain of paper and by closing time I'd gotten the backlog of work caught up. My "in" basket looked so nice when it was empty, and I left the office at five in a lighter mood than when I'd entered it that morning.

I decided to stop at Ken's Cigar Store at the corner of Kensington and Decarie to see if I could get a copy of yesterday's paper. I wanted to see the item that had been in on Kathleen Windsor. But Ken didn't have a copy left, so I picked up today's paper and thankfully took myself homeward, wondering if by chance there was anything in today's paper on the Windsor murder. It was a twenty-minute walk to school and I usually walked both ways for the exercise. Today my inclination was to hop on a bus, but I decided I needed some fresh air after being cooped up for four days. It was a mild day and a heavy, wet snow was falling, turning to gray slush as one walked on it.

When I got home I changed into pants and a sweater and sat down to peruse the paper. My eye scanned each page, but there wasn't a thing about the Windsor murder.

At five-thirty a friend of mine, Valerie Randolph, called and said she'd like to come over for a while tonight if I wasn't busy. She had something interesting to tell me, she told me in an excited voice. I had nothing scheduled for tonight except an early bedtime and I was as curious as the next person, so I told Valerie to come over and hung up, speculating whether what she had to tell me had anything to do with the smooth, expensive-looking character I'd met her with a week ago downtown. Valerie had introduced him as Paul Hanna and he'd looked me over with a connoisseur's eyes before flashing a well-practiced smile—which I had an idea was supposed to drop the ladies in their tracks. Valerie was on the rebound from a broken romance and I hoped she knew what she was doing. Paul Hanna was too old for her, too old and too smooth and too knowing. Well, I'd find out what it was all about in a few hours.

I was peeling potatoes for dinner when the door buzzer went. When I opened the door—with the chain on—there was Detective Lieutenant Noël Philippe, his long, bloodhound face looking more tired than ever. He doffed his battered gray hat, bowed slightly and asked if he could come in. He had a few questions to ask. I ushered him into the living room, wishing to God I had never heard of Kathleen Windsor. What could he want of me now? I'd told him everything I knew.

The detective sank languidly down on the sofa beside me and turned his world-weary gray eyes on me.

"When was the last time you saw George Matrai, mademoiselle?"

"George Matrai?" I was startled by the question. What could the janitor have to do—? "I can't think offhand . . . wait a minute . . . I actually haven't seen him since last Friday night when we took Kathleen Windsor home. I've been home with a cold the last four days. Today is the first day I've been out and I didn't notice him around coming or going. But you were talking to him last night. Why do you ask—?"

Lieutenant Philippe sighed heavily. "I ask, mademoiselle, because I would like to have another little talk with George Matrai. I spoke to him last night about six and he has not been seen since by anyone in the building. It appears that he has—how do you say that—flown the coop? Constable Rigaud and I took the liberty of entering his apartment just now and we found the bureau drawers in his bedroom empty of clothes and the cupboards empty of clothes. It seems that Mr. Matrai was upset by my visit last night."

I was puzzled. Why should George Matrai have taken flight? "But Lieutenant, what did you want with the janitor? He doesn't know any more than I do about Kathleen Windsor—if that's what you were calling on him about."

"I'm not so sure that he doesn't know more than you do about Kathleen Windsor. I decided to check him out and today at headquarters I received an interesting report. In the past five years George Matrai has served two prison terms for indecent assault on women." Lieutenant Philippe's voice was soft, but his face was grim. "If you recall, mademoiselle,

59

I informed you last night that Miss Windsor had been sexually molested."

A thrill of fear ran down my spine and I stared horrified at the detective. "You mean you think *he* killed Miss Windsor?"

"I know only that he merits investigation. The puzzling thing about the Windsor murder was how the killer got into the apartment. There was no sign of forced entry, which leads to the obvious conclusion that the murdered woman willingly admitted the murderer. Then we come to the question, Would she have opened her door to a stranger at that late hour—probably around midnight? From what I have learned of the late Kathleen Windsor, I take it she was a very immature and naïve woman. But weigh this against the fact she had been terrified earlier in the night because she was followed. So frightened she insisted that George Matrai search the apartment—even under the beds—for an intruder. Does it sound reasonable that a woman in this state of mind would open the door to a stranger at midnight?

"I can come to only one conclusion: Kathleen Windsor *knew* the person who came to her door late last Friday night. From talking to her mother, I gathered she led a very quiet, well-ordered life—one might say a very subdued life. She would not have the type of friends who came calling at midnight. And that brings us to George Matrai—the man who so obligingly escorted her home because she was frightened—the polite little man who was not sexually mature and who knew that Kathleen Windsor was alone in her apartment. After he got home that night, George may have sat and thought about it—until an idea formed in his aberrant mind. Then George might have gone back to the woman's apartment and gained admittance on the pretext that he wanted to be sure everything was all right. Naïve Kathleen Windsor would have let him in—completely unsuspecting."

A wave of nausea hit me and I put my head in my hands. Oh my God, had I, by asking the janitor to walk Kathleen home, sealed her death warrant? But it couldn't be, it couldn't be . . . not that quiet, good-natured little man who was always so polite.

"But Lieutenant, I don't believe he would do such a thing. He just wasn't the type to commit murder."

The detective sighed. "Mademoiselle, we have heard that phrase so often from the friends and families of murderers that we no longer look for types. Murderers come in all shapes and guises. Quite often, they are quiet, polite people —like George Matrai. What do you know of the man?"

"Not much, really. I've lived here a year and although I haven't had many real conversations with him, I got the impression he was courteous, rather retiring and a very good worker. He was Johnny-on-the-spot when you had a leaking faucet or a stuck window and he kept the lobby spotlessly clean. Last summer I often saw him working on the flower beds in front of the building. He would always smile in a shy, good-natured way and comment on the weather.

"Once, in the summer, I did get into a conversation with him when I remarked on the flowers. He told me he'd fled from Hungary in the 1956 uprising. He said it was terrible living in a police state and he was thankful every day of his life for the freedom he had here. George Matrai said he had nightmares of being deported to Hungary for some slight infraction of the law. Come to think of it, Lieutenant, maybe his fear of the police and of being deported was what made him do a disappearing act last night after you'd visited him."

Lieutenant Philippe rubbed the bag under one jaundiced eye and again sighed wearily. I was beginning to think he had tired blood.

"It is possible that fear and not guilt made George Matrai flee last night. Can you recall anything else he told you about himself?"

"Nothing I can think of at the moment . . . except he said he liked to take walks at night—" I stopped with another sudden sick sensation at the pit of my stomach.

A wry smile quirked one side of the detective's mouth. "I

have found people who take walks at night to be very interesting. The question is, mademoiselle, Did George Matrai take a walk after he'd brought Kathleen Windsor home last Friday? And did he take a walk on Winnicott Road the night the Grunberger woman was murdered?"

Lieutenant Philippe muttered something under his breath in French and I had the decided impression he was swearing.

"The only lead we have in the Windsor killing—and he is not to be found." He eased his slight frame out of the chair as though it weighed a ton. "We will stake out the janitor's apartment and, hopefully, the bird will return to the nest. I am sorry to have troubled you again, mademoiselle, but I thought it just possible the janitor might have come to you before leaving."

"It's quite all right, Lieutenant," I said, escorting him to the hall. But it wasn't all right at all. I was heartsick with the thought that I, in my efforts to assist Kathleen Windsor, might have introduced her to her killer.

At the door, the detective turned to me and said abruptly: "From what you know of Kathleen Windsor, would you think it likely that she had a lover?"

The question was so unexpected and so ludicrous I couldn't think of an answer for a moment; then I spoke with emphasis. "I suppose anything is possible, but having met Kathleen Windsor, I would find it hard to conceive of. Do the police think there could have been a lover involved?"

"We found a diary—well hidden from prying eyes. The entries in it dated from October to the twenty-third of this month. The diary was one long love letter to her dark-haired Steven. "We should have considered it more seriously," Lieutenant Philippe said dryly, "if we hadn't found three other diaries, devoted to Robin, Brian and Edward respectively. The diaries sound like the fantasies of a love-starved middle-aged woman. No one we have talked to so far has ever seen her with a man. Her murder, apparently, is the work of a sexual deviate, but still, the diaries are interesting. Tonight

62

I am going to talk to the members of St. Simon's Church choir." Lieutenant Philippe clapped his decrepit hat on the back of his black head and departed, bowing formally as I opened the door for him.

I went out to the kitchen and made myself a drink to take the edge off Lieutenant Philippe's visit. He had not been the bearer of glad tidings. I sipped my drink while I prepared dinner, one question endlessly chasing itself through my mind: Had I, by asking the janitor to walk Kathleen home, delivered her into the hands of her killer?

I was grateful when Laura came in twenty minutes later and I could unburden myself of the shocking news the detective had brought. Laura, though surprised to learn that George Matrai was a molester of women, reacted as I had to the idea that he might have returned to Kathleen Windsor's apartment last Friday night and murdered her.

"I can't believe it, Nicky. He was such a *nice* little man—so soft-spoken and obliging. He may have had convictions for indecent assault—although I've never heard of him annoying anyone in the building—but the lieutenant didn't say anything about him being violent in his assaults. And there's a difference between molesting and murder. Of course Philippe may be right about his theory that murderers don't run to type . . . but still, it's rather unbelievable. I think it's likely that George disappeared because the police frightened him. You, yourself, Nicky, were afraid of getting involved with the police. And remember, George Matrai was always afraid of being deported. But even if he did kill Kathleen, it won't do any good to blame yourself. Who would *dream* that our nice little janitor was dangerous?"

We dropped the subject then and turned to pleasanter topics. I told Laura that Valerie Randolph was coming down tonight and Laura said that right after dinner she was going to bake the birthday cake for Aunt Emily. A Schwarzwalder Kirschtorte was what she called it and I had to get her to translate. A Black Forest cherry cake, she enlightened me, and promised it would be a work of art. Laura has a soft spot for my Aunt Emily.

Valerie arrived at eight and I was glad of her company to take my mind off the depressing subject of murder. The brown eyes sparkled and the shining brown hair swung animatedly as she talked. She was as bubbly as champagne, and the cause of all the effervescence, as I had suspected, was none other than the suave-looking middle-aged man I'd met her with downtown last week.

"He's a real dream, Nicky. So smooth and sophisticated." She tossed her brown head disdainfully. "Peter seems utterly *crass* beside him!"

I had to suppress a smile. Her romance with Peter had been a four-alarm conflagration and she had deluged the ruins with her tears. And now Paul Hanna had entered the picture and Peter was suddenly *crass!* My amusement was tempered with concern though. Valerie was highly impressionable and easily swept off her feet. I didn't want to see her get burned in the fire Paul Hanna had lit.

"What's he do for a living, Val?"

"He's a TV producer. Can you imagine! Little Valerie Randolph going out with a real live TV producer?"

There was such awe in her voice that for a moment I thought she was talking about God.

"He knows musicians and show people and writers—simply *everybody!* And I could hardly wait to tell you, Nicky—he's going to get me a part in a TV play as soon as he can find one that's right for me. Doesn't it sound fabulous?"

It sounded fabulous all right. It also sounded awfully familiar. "And what will he do for an encore, Val?"

"What?" said Valerie, looking utterly deflated by my flippant response to her earth-shaking news.

"Don't mind me, Val, I'm just being cynical. But I didn't know you wanted to be a TV star. What happened to the vine-covered cottage and the three rosy cherubs you've been hankering after?"

64

"Oh, Paul's *crazy* about children, but right now he's married to this shrew of a wife and she doesn't understand him at *all*. He's working on a divorce, but these things take time. . . ."

Oh, sweet innocence, I thought, she thinks he wants to *marry* her! "But Val, isn't he a little old for you?"

"Old?" Her tone was lofty. "I don't measure age by the calendar, Nicky. He's in his *prime*—so knowledgeable, yet so vigorous and exciting in outlook. I just couldn't bear a younger man now. They're so . . . so crass."

Spoken like a true woman of the world, thought I to myself, wondering when I would be called upon to pick up the pieces. And called upon I would be, if I knew my Val. And if I knew my Paul Hannas. Entertainment people were high-voltage types and Val was decidedly low voltage. She might like the glamour and excitement of being seen around town with a TV personality, but when she found out she had to play house with Paul Hanna before she got to play in one of his TV productions, little Val would run for cover—all broken up over the perfidy of men. I might be mistaken in my impression of Paul Hanna, of course, but from where I sat, he had wheeler-dealer written all over him. And I knew better than to warn Valerie of the pitfalls. Unfortunately she was one of those girls who have to learn the hard way.

"Well, far be it from me to be a kill-joy, Val. 'Gather ye rosebuds, while ye may,' but please don't listen too hard for the peal of distant wedding bells until Paul Hanna actually gets his divorce. Sometimes they somehow never materialize."

I knew I was throwing ice water on a dream and Val responded by changing the subject a little huffily. She asked about Chris and then we talked about my upcoming trip to Jamaica. Later I got around to the subject of the two recent murders in the area and my involvement with the police over Kathleen Windsor. Val hadn't heard anything of the murders and she listened with a kind of frightened fascination, her earlier huffiness completely dissipated. I also told her about the attack on Laura on Monday night, and Val's expressive brown eyes mirrored her shock. I told her there was a policeman watching the park but I'd feel a lot better if she took a taxi home. It really wasn't safe for a woman to be out at night alone until the killer of Kathleen Windsor and Elsie Grunberger was caught. Somehow I had the feeling that the man who killed Kathleen and the other woman—and the man who had dragged Laura into the park—were one and the same. That let out George Matrai, of course.

Valerie agreed wholeheartedly with me on the taxi suggestion. As she put it, she would not set foot on the street alone at night while there was a maniac loose in the district.

Just then Laura called us into the kitchen to view her night's work—a huge dark beauty of a cake, glistening with shiny red maraschino cherries. While Val and I gazed at it covetously, Laura smiled and lifted its offspring from the oven—a miniature replica of the one we'd been eyeing longingly. Val and I broke into pleased smiles and Laura laughed.

"I had to have a tasting committee, girls, and I hoped you two would volunteer."

I put coffee on while Laura cleared up the mess from her baking and then the three of us sat in the kitchen eating Laura's Schwarzwalder Kirschtorte with great enthusiasm. Val and I pronounced it delicious and Laura looked well pleased with the verdict.

I called a taxi for Val just before eleven and Laura and I went down to the street when it arrived and saw Val safely inside. It had been Laura's idea to accompany me to the taxi with Val and I knew she felt as I did. That somewhere, very close to home, a psychopath was roaming the streets and it wasn't wise to leave the safety of the building alone after dark. I asked the taxi driver to escort his passenger into her apartment house and waved goodbye to Val. "I'll call you before I leave for Jamaica. Take care of yourself, Val!"

66

Chapter 9

Thursday went by in a rush. Miss Eden was heading up a
two-day teachers' conference at Braemar College next week
and I had endless directives and reports to type up, as well as
numerous phone contacts to make with teachers who would
be giving papers. But I had everything under control by four
o'clock—my usual quitting time—and left the school with the
satisfied feeling of having done a good day's work. I stopped
at Ken's Cigar Store for a paper and was pleased to find he
had gotten in a good selection of Christmas wrappings. I
could get my gift wrapping done tonight and that would be
one job taken care of before the scramble to get ready for
my trip to the Caribbean next week. I searched the paper
when I got home for any word on the Windsor murder but
drew a blank.

When Laura came home from work we had a fast supper of
macaroni and cheese and a salad and then she was off to her
class in restaurant administration. I hurried through the dishes,
washed my hair and went to work on the gift-wrapping chore,
my head turbaned in a towel. I was about halfway through
the job when Chris called. I told him about Lieutenant Philippe's visit last night and George Matrai's disappearance.
Chris gave a low whistle of surprise.

"So he folded his tent like the Arab and silently stole away.
It looks rather bad for Mr. Matrai, but it still doesn't mean
he's guilty. He may have gone to ground for no other reason
than that he was scared stiff by the police."

We tossed the subject around for a few minutes and then the conversation turned to tomorrow night's date.

"This comedy we're going to see is one of those *ménage à trois* things called *Three Is Cheaper than Two*. I can't say how good it is, but Guy knows the playwright and is anxious to see some of his work. We're all going to meet at your place and you can expect us around six. We won't have to leave for the theater until about seven-thirty, so I'll bring the makings for martinis. Do you think you could give us a little something to nibble on? We'll be pretty hungry by the time we get to Lisa's buffet after the show. But not too much: she's going to have a real spread."

I'd already thought of that and told Chris I'd provide something to allay the pangs of hunger. Then he surprised me by saying Guy wanted to know what color dress I'd be wearing: he was providing flowers for the ladies.

"The play's his treat and now flowers. Is it some special occasion, Chris?"

"According to Guy, it is. But he won't let me in on what it is. He says he'll make an announcement at supper tomorrow—so you'll have to contain your curiosity, Muffet. Now, what about the dress?"

I made up my mind in a hurry. The yellow silk with the scoop neckline would be right for an evening at the theater and Chris liked it on me. Could there be a better reason for wearing it?

"Yellow, Chris, yellow like in buttercups."

"Yellow like in *Crome Yellow*," the deep voice corrected. The love of my life, being a literary type, nearly always associates to books and fictional characters. But I don't care what he associates to as long as he remembers. And with all those imaginary people chasing themselves around his fertile brain, it's hard for him to remember mundane matters like the colors of dresses. I was going to ask him how his book was coming but thought better of it. Chris thought it was bad luck or something to talk about a book in progress and all I ever got when I did ask was a noncommittal "It's coming."

There was an amused note in his voice now. "How's Easy Rider these days?"

Easy Rider was Aunt Emily, of course. Chris got a big kick out of her and was always threatening to put her in a book. I told him about the two boys from the drop-in center and the birthday cake that Aunt Emily was going to pick up tomorrow.

"Tell her not to leave till I get there. I've got a kiss for her." The quiet voice dropped to a whisper that sent pleasurable shivers up my spine. "And a round dozen for you, Cleopatra." Then he said, "Yellow like in *Crome Yellow*," and hung up.

I went back to the gift wrapping with a singing heart; just hearing Chris's voice had that effect on me. And while I cut and folded paper and tied what I hoped were artistic bows, my mind zeroed in on the question "Should I marry Chris? I'd told him I'd give him a definite answer when I got back from Jamaica. And he'd told me firmly that he expected an answer then. Chris is a patient man, but he's not wishy-washy. And that didn't give me much time to make up my vacillating mind.

Was I being a fool to hesitate? Did I have to have the whole loaf? For that matter, wasn't half a loaf of the whole-grain-enriched variety better than a whole loaf of the doughy white ersatz article? Some of my friends had settled for the latter and were now in the process of getting divorced. Was I being an immature adolescent in wanting to be first and foremost in Chris's mind as well as in his heart? Wasn't his heart enough? The only rival I'd have to worry about was his typewriter. And wasn't it a little silly to be jealous of a machine when some women had to compete with flesh-and-blood rivals?

All the questions weren't bringing me any closer to a decision. I was going to let it wait until I got to the Caribbean.

I smiled and picked up the last gift to be wrapped—Chris's. It was an eighteen-inch-high carved wooden figure wearing a

69

metal helmet with the visor down and carrying a shield. I'd snatched it up when I'd discovered it in the Casa Bella in the Place Ville Marie a week ago because it was none other than my man's favorite fictional character—Don Quixote. As Chris had once told me, everybody tilts at windmills occasionally, but did anyone else do it with such *style!* I gave the melancholy wooden face a kiss, in lieu of Chris, and put it in a carton that had held an umbrella. I wrapped it in glittery brown paper, topped it with a gold bow and gave it another kiss. My gift wrapping was finished.

I toweled my hair dry, brushed it to a gleaming luster and got ready for bed. Laura came in just as I was going to my room and we talked for a few minutes. She said Norman Roxburgh had watched her all through class and had tried to waylay her as she left the building. She'd evaded him by jumping into a taxi that happened to be right out front. She'd spoken to the principal before class and arranged to be transferred to the other class in restaurant administration. It was held on the same nights but began and ended a half-hour later, so she would be able to avoid seeing Norman Roxburgh altogether. Laura said he'd become a little abusive when she'd jumped into the taxi and she felt a little frightened of him. I'd thought she seemed nervous when she came in. But who could blame her—with an obnoxious character bullying her at school and that terrifying attack in the park three nights ago. It would probably take her a little time to blot that evening from memory.

Chapter 10

As soon as I got home on Friday I had a quick shower, dressed and put on my make-up to leave the bathroom free for Laura when she dashed in at five-thirty. Julian was calling for her at six, which gave her only half an hour to get ready. I gave myself a last check in the long mirror in the bathroom, added a fine-gold-mesh bracelet to one slim yellow-sleeved arm and decided I was ready.

I was arranging sardines on crackers when Laura popped her head around the kitchen door, said, "Hi, talk to you later," and disappeared again. The dressed crackers were neatly arranged on two platters and I was filling a cut glass bowl with olives when the door buzzer went.

It was Julian Brooks, looking youthful and attractive in a narrowly cut royal blue coat, which set off his fair skin and dark blond hair. I ushered him into the living room, told him Laura was not quite ready and that I'd be in to keep him company in a few minutes.

I'd finished my preparations in the kitchen when the door buzzer pealed again. As I passed through the living room on my way to the hall, I noticed that Julian was absorbed in sketching something on a small pad of paper. I was surprised when I opened the door to find Aunt Emily with two boys in tow. She hadn't said anything about bringing the boys with her.

"Hello, dear," she piped. "Hope you don't mind me bringing the boys. They were coming in just as I was leaving my apartment and I thought it would be nice for them to meet you."

She looked at the tall, gangling boy with the shock of wheat blond hair and said, "This is Donald Hammill." Then she indicated the undernourished-looking boy with the thin weasel face and sullen expression and said, "Tony Bartha."

Donald grinned and said, "Hi," shifting the big guitar over one shoulder, while Tony looked at me with a scowl on his face and barely nodded. I could see why Aunt Emily wasn't much taken with Tony Bartha.

I shepherded the trio into the living room and introduced them to Julian Brooks, who looked just a shade startled by the sight of Aunt Emily in plum velvet knickers, white silk socks and a white silk blouse with ruffles of lace at throat and wrists. It was probably my aunt's notion of proper attire for a birthday party, but she looked to me like a transplanted court page. I told her Laura would be out in a few minutes to present the birthday cake, and Aunt Emily said if I didn't mind, they'd wait to see Chris before leaving.

"You've got orders to wait for him. He has a kiss to give you. And I want you all to have a drink with us in honor of Donald's birthday when Chris gets here."

Aunt Emily looked pleased when I made this announcement, Donald looked at me shyly and blushed and Tony looked nowhere in particular with a surly scowl on his face. I got the idea that Tony Bartha thought birthday cakes were kid stuff. He plunked himself into a chair away from the main grouping of sofas and chairs, and Aunt Emily and Donald made themselves comfortable on floor cushions by the coffee table. Julian immediately jumped up, aghast at seeing an elderly lady on the floor.

"Do sit beside me, Mrs. Teasdale; the floor can't be very—"

"It's all right, Julian," I interrupted. "Aunt Emily likes sitting on the floor."

Just then Guy and Lisa Sabourin arrived, both of them in festive mood. Lisa, incidentally, is a statuesque blonde with

72

a Valkyrian profile. She looks regal any time, but tonight she was magnificent with her thick honey blond hair arranged in a coronet atop her queenly head, her Earth Mother figure draped in a shimmering maxi-length dark mink. They made a striking couple, with Guy's lean, dark, satyr face complementing Lisa's opulent blondness.

Guy gave me a kiss on the cheek and handed me a small florist's box with instructions to put it in the frig till we were ready to leave.

There were more introductions in the living room and then we all settled down to wait for Chris and Laura to put in an appearance. Aunt Emily's bird-bright eyes went from Julian Brooks to Guy Sabourin, shrewdly sizing them up. Then she turned to me.

"Did you know somebody's watching your building, Nicky? I saw a man hidden in the trees bordering the lane. Wouldn't have even seen him if he hadn't moved slightly."

I was puzzled at first and a bit frightened. Then I remembered. "Oh, it's probably the police on the lookout for George Matrai."

Aunt Emily didn't know about this development of course, and for that matter, I discovered that Guy and Lisa knew nothing at all of the murders. For their benefit I told the full story of the two murders on Winnicott Road, Kathleen Windsor's visit to our apartment the night she was murdered, the subsequent visits of Lieutenant Philippe and the disappearance of the janitor. That led to a discussion of the murders, and neither Guy nor Lisa went along with Lieutenant Philippe's theory that Kathleen Windsor had willingly opened her door to her killer because she knew him. They both thought, like Chris, that a stranger could have gained admittance by a ruse. It seemed even more plausible to them in the light of Kathleen's naïveté.

Aunt Emily told us that a detective had visited the choir on Wednesday night and questioned the members about Kathleen Windsor. "Looked like he needed vitamins," she added.

That would have been Lieutenant Philippe, of course. Aunt Emily had thought it a little funny when the lieutenant had asked if any of them had ever seen Kathleen Windsor with a man.

"Why did you think that question funny, Mrs. Teasdale?" asked Guy.

"If you'd met her, Mr. Sabourin, you'd know. She just wasn't grown up enough to attract a man and she was really *afraid* of them—got all embarrassed and giggly when they were around. Of course some man might be attracted to her money. She had an income of fifteen thousand dollars a year from her father. Her mother paid all the expenses of the apartment, so she must have been able to put a tidy sum in the bank. But anyway, the only time I ever saw her alone with a man was that Sunday after church when she left early and I did too. He was most likely a friend of the family, but the detective told us to tell him everything we knew—no matter how unimportant it seemed—so I told him about seeing Kathleen get into a car with a man. He wanted to know what the man looked like. I couldn't give a very good description because I only caught a quick glimpse of him sideways. All that registered was black hair that covered his ears and one of those pointy little devil beards—like Mr. Sabourin wears."

Guy grinned. "A Vandyke, Mrs. Teasdale, or a spade beard, if you will, but please don't call it a little devil beard. You'll frighten my wife."

Aunt Emily favored Guy with a long inquisitive stare. "You *do* look a little like Satan, Mr. Sabourin, but if it makes you feel better, I'll call it a Vandyke."

Everybody but Tony was trying to suppress a laugh, but Aunt Emily, completely unaware of the amusement she was causing, went on with her story.

"Anyways, I told the detective about the man in the car and then he wanted to know if Kathleen had ever made up stories. One doesn't like to speak ill of the dead, but the policeman was trying to find her murderer and we all had to

74

help. Everybody in the choir told the detective that Kathleen had made up stories something fierce. In the ten years I knew her, she told me at least half a dozen tales of love affairs that ended in tragedy. Poor soul, it was all in her head."

Aunt Emily's nervously roving gaze lighted on the coffee table and she reached over and picked up the pad Julian had been drawing on. She held it up and peered at it intently. "That's a right pretty ship," she said, turning the pad toward the four of us on the sofa. It was a sketch of a sailing ship done in vermilion ink, its clouds of canvas billowing in an imaginary wind. At the bowsprit was the figure of an angel blowing a trumpet.

"Like it, Mrs. Teasdale?" said Julian with enthusiasm. "That's the *Flying Cloud,* a clipper ship."

"A right pretty name too. Seems to me I saw a picture of a ship just like that lately . . . but where—" Aunt Emily frowned in concentration.

Julian looked thoughtful for a moment. Then he said, "Ever been in the Warwick Tea room on Decarie, Mrs. Teasdale?"

"That's it, Mr. Brooks. I go there sometimes after church on Sunday for lunch and they've got a whole wall of drawings of tea clippers done in red ink."

"That's right, Mrs. Teasdale. I've been there myself. Beautiful ships, those clippers. Did you see the sketches of the *Thermopylae* and the *Cutty Sark?* They were great ships and great rivals. The *Cutty Sark* was the most powerful of the tea clippers but not quite as fast as the *Thermopylae.*" Julian glanced from face to face to see if he was holding our interest and then launched into a fascinating discourse on the famous China tea clippers of the 1800s.

We listened intrigued while Julian, his face aglow with fervor, drew a vivid word picture of the graceful China clippers, some of them with a delicate, almost fragile beauty of line. He reeled off name after magic name: *Flying Spur, Fiery Cross, Sir Lancelot, Ariel;* pictured for us Pagoda anchorage at Foochow, where the great clippers assembled to load tea, all glistening with fresh paint, snow-white decks, glittering brass and burnished copper. He told us about the excitement of the tea races, the great Clyde builders, and Donald McKay, the American ship designer and builder who had built the renowned *Lightning*. He was back to his first loves, the *Cutty Sark* and the *Flying Cloud,* when the buzzer sounded again. Guy went to answer it. Julian looked at the rest of us guiltily.

"I say, I didn't mean to go on like that. I hope I haven't bored everyone."

We quickly assured him he hadn't. That on the contrary we'd found it fascinating. All except Tony Bartha, who sat hunched up in his chair, staring morosely at nothing, and Donald, who was cradling his guitar in both arms like a baby and looking lovingly at it. I could almost hear him crooning to it.

Guy came back a moment later, followed by Chris, who saluted the assembled company, winked at me and made a beeline for Aunt Emily. He stooped down and planted a kiss on the top of her head.

"I've waited a long time for that, Easy Rider," he said, grinning down at her.

"And I've waited half an hour for you, Christopher Galloway, and all I get is a kiss on the top of the head." She grinned at me impudently. "But I know you're afraid of making Nicky jealous."

Chris lowered his big frame to the floor beside her and the two of them bantered together like the old friends they were. The rest of us listened in amusement.

Laura finally put in an appearance a few minutes after Chris arrived and Julian Brooks got to his feet, a look of admiration on his thin, sensitive face. And the admiration was warranted. Laura was stunning in a deep-throated green wool that clung to the curves and looked great on the straight too. The soft color of her dress set off to perfection her shining fall of coppery hair and accentuated the beauty of her wide green eyes. Laura always wore green when she wanted to impress somebody.

Guy, who had been exchanging secret little smiles of satisfaction with Lisa ever since they'd arrived, jumped to his feet and orated: "A blonde, a brunette and a redhead! Gentlemen! We have all died and gone to heaven!" Then he sat down and slapped his knee in appreciation of his own wit. Lisa favored him with the fond, indulgent smile she reserved for him when he was being humorous.

Chris smiled broadly and picked up the brown bag he'd deposited on a table when he came in. "I think Guy needs a drink to steady him, Nicky. Want to help play bartender?"

I smiled and prepared to do my duty. I asked everybody's preference and reported to Chris in the kitchen: three martinis, two manhattans, four Dubonnets.

When we had everything ready, Chris carried the drinks into the living room while I took the two platters of hors d'oeuvres. Chris proposed a toast to Donald and we all drank standing, Donald looking embarrassed and pleased at all the attention. Tony looked as though his drink were sour. Before Donald could sit down again, Guy suggested he give us a little concert on his guitar. Donald flushed and turned his earnest cornflower blue eyes on Aunt Emily with an unspoken plea.

"You can do it, Donald," she encouraged him. "Just one or two songs, then we'll leave."

"Come on, Donald," urged Lisa, "we're all friends."

Donald brushed a swatch of hair out of his eyes, moved to the center of the floor reluctantly and started picking at his guitar. He strummed a few random chords and then seemed to gather confidence from the throbbing strings. A few more runs and he segued into "Wildhearts and Wildflowers," singing in a husky baritone that gained power as he went. In a minute we were all tapping feet in time with the pulsing beat of the music he was coaxing from his big, country-style guitar, his body swaying now with the sound. We had barely time to applaud at the end of the piece when he swung into "The

Moon for My Lamp," completely unaware of his audience now. The big hands caressed the strings, wooing gut-deep emotion from the heart of his instrument and we were deep in nostalgia country when the lover's fingers came to rest. Then we were on our feet applauding, urging, "one more." Donald, smiling shyly, looked at Aunt Emily.

"The boys and girls from the drop-in center are coming at eight for Donald's party, but I guess we have time for just one more. What about 'City of Night,' Donald? He composed it himself," Aunt Emily told us proudly.

"'City of Night,' let it be," said Chris.

Donald shifted from one long leg to the other, played a series of lighthearted chords that changed to deep-throated melancholy as he commenced "City of Night." The vulnerable young face was a study in sadness as he sang in his strong, compelling voice:

> "Asphalt and concrete, neon and steel,
> Nowhere, nowhere anything real.
> Bolted doors on the houses,
> Shuttered doors on the hearts,
> Broken dreams in the concrete,
> Murdered dreams in the steel.
> Grief in the darkness, grief and despair,
> Nowhere, nowhere, someone to care."

It was a modern lament, simple and direct—and it pulled at the heartstrings. We listened in silence while Donald moved into the chorus, singing the words as though they were a prayer:

> "Got to get out of this City of Night
> Find me, oh find me, my City of Light."

The prayer died into silence that dissolved into the larger silence in the crowded room. Then the men were up shaking hands with Donald—subdued now and solemn. His heart had been in that song. Suddenly I noticed with dismay that Donald's mouth was trembling. Chris put an arm around him and steered him toward the kitchen door with a "Come on, Donald, let's have a look at that fabulous cake of yours."

Aunt Emily, who hadn't noticed the incident, came up to me a moment later to say she and the boys had better be going. I told her Donald was a little upset and had gone into the kitchen with Chris. We'd better wait till they came out. While we waited for them to return I glanced around the room. Laura was talking to Guy and Chris, and Julian was in earnest conversation with Lisa. He seemed to be thoroughly enjoying himself. Tony Bartha caught my eye when I glanced at him. Was it my imagination or was there a hint of insolence in the pale, dull eyes that stared at me from the sharp face?

Chris and Donald returned a few minutes later, Donald composed now and smiling a little sheepishly. I told Laura Aunt Emily had to leave and she went out to pack the birthday cake.

Guy got on his feet and offered to drive Aunt Emily and the boys home, not knowing they lived so close. Aunt Emily told him she lived at the corner of Winnicott and Côte St. Luc—just five minutes' walk away. Chris kidded that Guy was getting too interested in his girl, and Aunt Emily beamed, basking in the male attention she was getting.

We all went to the door to say goodbye to them, Tony carrying the cake in a hatbox and looking ineffably bored. I accompanied the trio to the lobby door and we arrived just as T. Oliphant came in, his bald dome a sickly color under the fluorescent lighting. The opaque eyes glared at me a fraction of a second; then they moved to Aunt Emily and traveled quickly down to her knees. Aunt Emily's long cape was open, revealing her knickers. T. Oliphant stared at her knickers a moment, then hurried past us, his eyes averted now, his mouth drawn in a tight pucker. I was glad to get back inside my apartment, away from that cadaverous apparition with the glittery eyes. The man was positively creepy!

79

Julian and Laura left right after Aunt Emily and the boys and the four of us remaining decided we had time for another drink before the theater. Guy had seen Donald crying and commented on it to Chris.

"His old man was a drunkard who beat up on him every time he had too much to drink—which was most of the time. Donald wrote that song 'City of Night' when he was living at home and feeling pretty low. And as he put it, everything was a bit much for him tonight: Aunt Emily taking him in and being so good to him and Laura baking a birthday cake for him and all of us applauding his guitar playing and singing. Donald's just not used to people being nice to him. He's a good kid, but he's pretty confused. He needs a man to straighten him out."

"I didn't care for that Tony Bartha," Lisa said. "How did those two ever get together?"

"Tony Bartha looked like bad news to me. I wish Aunt Emily would get rid of him." That was Chris, frowning at his martini glass.

"I think she will," I said. "She told me she didn't like him."

"Well, let's hope it's soon. He's not a good influence on Donald." Chris picked up a cracker spread with cheese and olives and turned to Guy.

"You and Lisa look like the cats that swallowed the canary tonight. Why don't you break down and tell us what the big secret is?"

Guy pushed his long black hair back from one cheek and smiled his satyr smile. "Not until we break out the champagne bottle tonight. The announcement warrants champagne and I think right now we'd better get moving if we're going to make the opening curtain."

Chris and I sighed in resignation and got up. Lisa gave us a serene, self-contained smile. Whatever it was, it must be good. When we were ready to leave, Guy pinned my corsage on my coat: a trio of tiny tea roses, whose delicate shadings of coral, orange and gold reminded me of a sunrise. When he had it firmly anchored, Guy stood back and grinned at me.

"Hope it looks as well on your dress, Nicky. I asked Chris what color it was and he said, 'Aldous Huxley.'" He punched Chris on the arm and laughed heartily. "I had a hell of a time finding a rose to go with Aldous Huxley."

Chapter 11

Lisa and I swung around on our stools to face Chris and Guy—standing behind us in the crowded bar of the Planet Theater. The curtain had just rung down on Act Two of *Three Is Cheaper than Two,* and Guy had suggested that a drink was in order if the third act was going to be as bad as the first two. Our discussion of the play—billed as a side-splitting comedy—occasioned a lot more laughter among us than had the performance so far. It was appallingly bad.

"When does the comedy start?" Chris wanted to know.

"Don't ask embarrassing questions, Christopher. What I want to know is which two were the husband?"

"You mean which one, don't you, dear? I counted two wives for sure—I think."

"I got things confused myself," said Chris dryly. "And if there's been any humor in that comedy so far, it was too sick to be recognized."

"Sicker," retorted Guy, rattling the ice cubes in his glass.

"Moribund," chorused Lisa. "Let's bury it."

"Rest in peace," I chimed in, and we clinked glasses, laughing merrily at our own wit. Or was it a touch of hysteria induced by the performance on stage?

Lisa's fabulous mink slipped from her shoulders and Guy bent over to anchor it, his pointy little devil beard just touching her coronet of honey blond hair. "Are you tired, dear?" he asked solicitously.

"I'm only tired of *Three Is Cheaper than Two*. How does everybody else feel about it?"

It turned out, after a small consultation, that everybody felt the same way Lisa did. It was just that no one wanted to be the first to suggest leaving. We all agreed we couldn't expect a third act miracle and left the theater, our high spirits undampened by the failure of the play.

"Ben Carter really bombed on that one," Guy commented as we walked up the street to the parking lot at the next corner. "If he can get that produced, there's hope for me."

Guy Sabourin, who has a full-time job as salesman for Drake Distilleries, is a playwright by night. In five years of writing he succeeded in having only one play produced—with so-so notices. Nothing daunted, he burns the midnight oil over his scripts, dreaming of the day when he can earn enough money from his plays to give up his job as salesman and devote full time to writing. Chris thinks he is being unrealistic. You can't earn a living from playwrighting, Chris said, unless you are lucky enough to attract the attention of the movie people. Chris just managed to support himself from writing novels and he supplemented his income by teaching creative writing at the university two nights a week. But in his case there's more reason to be optimistic. He has had three novels published and is becoming known—as witnessed by the climbing sales of his books.

There was an undercurrent of resentment in Guy's attitude toward Chris—for all his surface geniality. Occasionally his affable veneer cracked and Guy's resentment of Chris's success was exposed. Neither Chris nor I felt too comfortable with Guy Sabourin at times. He was too genial, too jovial— too much of the time. It didn't ring true somehow. When the mask slipped and Guy let go with a poison-tipped arrow,

82

it was almost a relief. I had the feeling sometimes that some-where behind the benevolent exterior he presented to the world, Guy Sabourin concealed a bulging quiver of poison-tipped arrows. But for most of the time he held his fire.

Chris said Guy controlled his hostility as well as he did because he had an inordinate desire to be liked and admired. Hence the debonair charm, the expansive gestures. Like the roses tonight, for example, the vintage wines he always served his guests, the lavish tips and the too-expensive Christmas gifts.

He was walking ahead of Chris and me, supporting Lisa with a firm arm. It was colder tonight and the morning's rain had coated the streets with treacherous patches of ice. I stepped along cautiously, Chris steadying me when I slipped. I was still thinking of Guy. Although he might present a Janus face to the world, there was nothing two-faced about his feelings for Lisa. He virtually worshiped the ground she walked on. Nothing was too good for her. Guy would mort-gage his soul to get Lisa something she wanted. And I couldn't help but wonder if he *hadn't* mortgaged his soul to buy the gorgeous mink Lisa was wearing. I knew he did pretty well as a salesman for Drake Distilleries: Guy had the personality that made a terrific salesman. But did he do *that* well?

At the entrance to the parking lot the four of us said hail and farewell again and agreed to meet at Guy and Lisa's apartment on Pine. Guy's new Mercedes-Benz slid out of the lot just ahead of Chris's green Ford. We kept the car in view for half a dozen blocks and then lost it when we had to stop for a traffic light.

In fifteen minutes we were at Lisa's apartment, a one-floor walk-up in an old converted mansion. It's Victorian through and through, with tall, narrow windows, leaded panes, thick oak doors and paneling and three-feet-deep win-dow seats. Guy was at the door to welcome us and usher us into the living room after we'd shed coats and boots in the hall. It's a beautiful place to come into out of the cold, bear-

83

ing the stamp of Lisa's opulent aliveness. Massive furniture in dark glowing woods, ruby red sofa and draperies, bibelots on every table and wall shelf, flowers everywhere in silver and glass containers. I was admiring Lisa's collection of hand-blown glass vases and pitchers when she appeared in the living room and announced there would be food in half an hour. I offered to help in the kitchen, but Lisa rejected my offer. One woman per kitchen was enough, she said. I was to sit and be lazy and enjoy myself. So while Lisa toiled over a hot stove, Guy and Chris and I sat sipping drinks and performing a post mortem on *Three Is Cheaper than Two*. We had finished our dissection of the play and were about to give the corpse a decent burial when Lisa announced that dinner was ready. She had gone all out to create a special meal, and the long refectory table in her dining room and been turned into a rijstafel or "rice table," lavishly spread with platters of rice and Madras Chicken Curry, and side dishes of mango and other chutneys, fried eggplant cubes, fresh pineapple cubes, peanuts and fried ripe bananas. To eat with the curry, Lisa had baked the traditional Indian bread, Chapati, and served it piping hot from the oven. We fell on the feast with zesty appetites, heaping praise on Lisa between mouthfuls.

How, I asked Lisa in amazement, had she come up with a spread like that in half an hour. She laughed and told me the secret was to start work on it first thing in the morning. Halfway through our meal, Guy left the table and returned carrying a bottle of champagne. He was beaming at everybody in general and Lisa in particular.

"Very special champagne, for a very special occasion," Guy said, holding up the bottle.

Chris smiled good-humoredly. "If you don't let us in on the secret and end the suspense in one minute flat, I'm going to break that bottle of champagne right over your head."

Guy pretended to be alarmed. He opened the bottle hastily, snatched up a wine glass and started pouring. "I should," he said, winking at Lisa, "be able to fill four glasses in one minute flat if I work fast."

When we all had glasses of champagne in front of us, Guy stood up at his place at the table, held his wine glass high and proclaimed:

"Ladies and gentlemen, a toast to my beautiful wife, Lisa, who is about to make me a father."

Chris and I stood up with Guy, gave a rousing cheer and downed the contents of our glasses. In all the excitement Guy's announcement had generated, Lisa sat quietly, looking infinitely pleased with herself. Guy looked at his wife with adoration in his eyes. Then he turned to Chris, an expression of mock alarm on his face again.

"Three *is* cheaper than two, isn't it, Chris?"

"You're going to find out, fellow, you're going to find out."

This set the tone for some lighthearted banter on the pleasures and perils of parenthood. When the party broke up a couple of hours later, we were still in high spirits. But when I was fixing my make-up in Lisa's bedroom, I caught a sober, worried look on her face.

"You look so serious, Lisa. Are you having second thoughts about having a baby?"

"Oh no, Nicky, I'm thrilled about it . . . it's just that . . ." She frowned, "Well, to tell the truth, I'm a little worried about Guy's lavish spending. The mink he bought me must be worth seven thousand dollars. And that on top of a Mercedes-Benz which he couldn't have got under twelve thousand. He told me he got a bonus for ranking as top salesman of the year, but I didn't think Drake Distilleries paid that kind of money out in bonuses. When I tried to pin Guy down about the bonus, he just told me not to worry my pretty little head about money."

I didn't know what to say. Guy's story sounded a little suspicious to me, but I didn't want to add to Lisa's worry. "If Guy isn't worrying, you shouldn't either," I said lightly.

85

"The mink looks stunning on you, Lisa. Why not just enjoy it?"

The frown erased itself from Lisa's forehead. "Maybe you're right, Nicky. But I just hope Guy hasn't gone into debt to buy it. With the baby coming, there's going to be added expense and he's going to find out three *isn't* cheaper than two!"

Chapter 12

I didn't wake up till nearly noon on Saturday and then I spent another twenty minutes lazily luxuriating in a warm cocoon of blankets while an icy wind from the open window set the curtains flailing about as though they were fighting an invisible foe. I lay curled in a ball with the blankets over my nose and thought of a lot of things. Of last night's date and Christopher Galloway first and foremost, and how I'd felt when I'd been with him. The way I always felt when I was with him—warm and alive and contented. I saw the strong, masculine face, the thick brown hair curling slightly above his ears, the deep-set blue eyes looking into mine as he'd kissed me last night. Could I bear to give him up? I hugged the pillow in a sudden ecstasy of emotion. No way, I whispered into the pillow. Somehow I had to come to terms with Chris's commitment to writing.

I thought of Guy Sabourin and the small frown of worry that had creased Lisa's smooth forehead when she'd talked about the mink. First a Mercedes-Benz, then a maxi-length mink of the choicest skins. Around twenty thousand dollars

86

for the two prestige items. Where was Guy getting that kind of money?

And Tony Bartha. What was that sullen, sly-looking character doing with Donald Hammill, a boy who looked like he should be striding through a prairie wheat field with a blade of grain in his teeth?

And was that man we'd seen in the trees by the apartment building really the police? Somehow it seemed odd that they should still be watching for George Matrai. He'd disappeared last Wednesday. Did the police still hope he'd come back? It was a week since Kathleen Windsor's murder and eleven days since the Grunberger murder. Had the police come up with anything or were there going to be two more unsolved murders on the books?

I suddenly decided to stop asking myself unanswerable questions, jumped out of bed and closed the window. I passed Laura in the hall on my way to the kitchen for breakfast. She'd just finished brunch, she informed me, but would join me for a cup of coffee.

I was finishing off my second blueberry pancake when Laura breezed into the kitchen, looking positively aglow. Her date with Julian Brooks had gone well, I decided. She poured coffee for both of us and sat down opposite me, her big green eyes sparkling. I grinned at her.

"I take it you didn't suffer too much last night?"

Laura grinned back at me, then spoke in that carefully flippant tone she sometimes assumes to conceal her real feelings. "The only thing that suffered was Julian's wallet."

"Where did you go?"

"To the Bluenose Inn for dinner. Julian suggested it and I could see why after we were talking awhile. It's named after the fastest schooner to sail the North Atlantic and it turned out that Julian is mad about boats."

I laughed. "We discovered that last night while you were in the bathroom making yourself glamorous for him. He gave us a fascinating talk on China tea clippers—seemed to know just about everything there was to know about them. And his face was lit with the fervor of the fanatic while he talked."

"He didn't mention China clippers, but no doubt he'll get to that. He gave me the history of the *Bluenose* and a rundown on sailboats, catamarans, runabouts—if it floated, Julian talked about it. And especially he talked about his own twenty-nine-foot sloop, which is now sleeping the winter away in storage. The *Swallow* is Julian's pride and joy—and according to him the most beautiful sloop ever to sail the St. Lawrence. He said he bought Hood sails for it last year and I wasn't too impressed—not knowing anything about sails—until he told me they were a Dior brand to yachtsmen. Worth a mink coat apiece."

I smiled at Laura over my coffee cup. "You must feel a little waterlogged after all the nautical talk."

She tapped ash from her cigarette with a slim lacquered fingertip. "Not a bit of it. We went to Oliver's after dinner for the music and talked about everything under the sun. Julian's a lovely dancer."

"Then you did have a good time?"

"Wonderful, Nicky. He's a very nice guy. Quiet and a little shy but full of boyish enthusiasm about everything. A nice change from some of the jaded, sophisticated types in town. And a nice change from Norman Roxburgh. Julian is a gentleman."

"Are you seeing him again?"

"We're going out next Friday." There was that carefully casual tone of voice again. Laura, I thought, really liked Julian Brooks but was keeping her enthusiasm banked for fear of getting burned again. She hadn't yet recovered from her broken romance with Carl.

"How did your evening go, Nicky?"

"Fine. The play was a dud and we left before it was over, but Lisa had a delicious curry dinner for us and very special champagne."

88

"Champagne yet! What was the occasion? Or does Guy Sabourin always have to impress people?"

"I'm afraid he always has to impress people. But it *was* a special occasion. Lisa's going to have a baby and Guy thought the news was worth a celebration. He was as proud as a peacock."

"How does Lisa feel about it?"

"She can hardly wait. She was made to be a mother. But talking about impressing people, in honor of the coming event, Guy bought Lisa a magnificent dark mink—maxi-length, if you please. And just a month ago he bought a Mercedes-Benz. Laura thinks the one he bought cost about twelve thousand dollars and she said the mink must be worth seven thousand anyway."

Laura raised a finely arched eyebrow. "Did a rich uncle die and leave him a small fortune?"

"No, and that's what's worrying Lisa. She doesn't know where he got the money. He told her he got a nice bonus lately for being top salesman of the year and she shouldn't worry her pretty little head about mundane money matters. Lisa says Guy has earned bonuses before, but she didn't think Drake Distilleries paid bonuses that would cover a mink and a car. She's afraid he's gone into debt. And with the baby coming, there isn't any money to throw around."

"Well, maybe the responsibilities of being a father will make Guy Sabourin grow up a little. He acts like a show-off kid. By the way, Nicky, did you see anyone in the shadow of the building when you came in this morning?"

"Yes, a man was standing in among the trees by the lane and I wondered about it. I mean, it's a little scary coming in late at night and finding someone hiding there watching the building. It *is* the police, isn't it?"

Laura frowned. "You said they were staking out George Matrai's apartment, but wouldn't that mean they'd have a man *inside* his apartment? It seems to me having a man outside

89

wouldn't be as effective. They could miss him going in in the dark. What about checking with that Lieutenant Philippe?"

I set my coffee cup down and got up from the table. "I think I will, Laura. It won't do any harm to ask. I don't know if Lieutenant Philippe will be in his office this Saturday, but it's worth a try."

It turned out that Lieutenant Philippe was in his office and a little disappointed to learn that I was calling to ask for information, not give it. In his soft-spoken Gallic voice, with a hint of surprise in it, he informed me:

"No, mademoiselle, we do not have a man on George Matrai's apartment now. We took him off yesterday morning, and in any case, he was planted inside the apartment, not outside the building."

I felt a slight quiver of apprehension in the region of my spine. "Then who is it, Lieutenant? Somebody's watching the building."

There was a long pause at the other end of the line. "When did you see him there, mademoiselle?"

"My aunt noticed him last night around six, my apartmentmate saw him when she came in around one this morning and I saw him at three this morning."

"I trust that you and your friend did not come home alone?"

"No, of course not. Both of us have been coming home with someone or in taxis since that attack on Laura. But what about this man?" A frightening thought struck me. "Lieutenant, it could even be the man who attacked Laura. We couldn't see his face in the darkness. He was well back in the trees. Could it be *him*, waiting for Laura to come in alone?"

"I do not think so, mademoiselle. I do not think your friend's assailant would dare to attack her outside an apartment building where help could swiftly be summoned. But we will investigate. We will send a man down and I think you will find by tonight that your man in the trees has disappeared."

"Thank you, Lieutenant," I said, relieved that action

90

would be taken. Two murders and the attack on Laura had made me a little less than unflappable.

Laura looked a little startled when I told her the man watching the building was not the police; relieved when I told her the police would investigate. She too, it seemed, was a little less than unflappable after that terrifying incident in the park last Monday.

If I was going to get that peony-pink dress made up for my trip to Jamaica this weekend, there was no time to waste. I dressed in a hurry, whipped my room into order and went out for the week's groceries. I arrived back at the building at two-thirty and stopped at the mailbox. I was returning to the apartment with a handful of envelopes when Sybil Hepworth's door opened and she bore down on me, her ample bosom quivering with suppressed excitement. She opened with the weather, as usual.

"Good morning, Miss Nugent. It's a cold day, isn't it? We're going to have snow tonight." Her voice dropped to an excited whisper. "Have you ever noticed that tall, thin man who comes in to visit Miss Barrette in Number Nine? The one she says is her brother?"

I saw the gleam of malice in Sybil's piglike eyes and didn't wait for any more. "Excuse me, Miss Hepworth, I'm expecting a phone call any minute." Her puffy face was a study in petulance as I breezed past her, my apartment key at the ready. How long would it take that malicious woman to realize I wasn't interested in her gossip?

I spent the rest of the afternoon working on my dress, interrupted by one call from Aunt Emily, who phoned to tell Laura how much they'd enjoyed her cake. Then she wanted to talk to me. She spent half an hour talking about the party they'd had for Donald and about the girls and boys who'd come from the drop-in center. Donald had played his guitar and they'd rapped around the clock, as Aunt Emily put it. She remarked again that Donald had a lot of soul. He thought Chris was a great guy and he hoped he'd meet him again.

Then my aunt got onto the subject of Tony Bartha and I didn't like what I heard. She'd seen him hanging around Crestview Public School on several occasions and wondered what a boy of nineteen would want with youngsters of public school age. And once she'd seen him talking to a flashily dressed man standing by a Cadillac on Côte St. Luc. Tony had abruptly moved away from the man when he'd spotted Aunt Emily, and when she'd asked who the man was, Tony said he was just giving him directions. The Bartha boy, she said, was too cynical and knowing for his age and what worried her most of all was that Donald seemed a little uncomfortable around him—almost as though he was a little afraid of Tony. I remembered what Aunt Emily had said about Donald dallying with Mary Jane and Tony going steady with her.

"Do you think Tony is supplying Donald with drugs?" Aunt Emily.

"Not now, dear. I think he may have given Donald something once or twice, but Donald is certainly not on drugs now. He's too lively and alert."

I had to agree with my aunt there. Fresh-faced, clear-eyed Donald couldn't possibly be taking drugs. Then something else occurred to me. "Do you think Tony could be dealing drugs to school children?"

"I thought of that, Nicky. I searched his belongings one day while he was out. Couldn't find anything, but I'm still suspicious. Whatever he's doing, something about him tells me he's not on the level. And he's not good for Donald. I'm telling Tony tonight he has to leave on Monday. That will give him a little time to find somewhere to go. He can always sleep at the drop-in center for a few nights and they try to find them places to stay if they're not underage."

"But isn't Donald underage? He didn't look more than sixteen to me."

"He was sixteen yesterday. And his case is being investigated by the juvenile authorities and the police. They try to

92

get the boys to return home if conditions are favorable, and if they aren't they put them in homes for boys. In Donald's case the authorities don't want to return him to his home against his will because the environment is too unhealthy for a young boy. His name is on the list for a supervised boys' home and I've permission to keep him until they find a place for him. He's really a sweet boy and I'm going to miss him when he goes."

"Well, I'm glad to hear you're getting rid of Tony. None of us here last night liked him one bit."

There was a long silence on the other end of the line and I said, "Aunt Emily?" There was still silence. She must be listening for vibes again. I waited patiently. Her voice when it came through was a thin treble.

"I'm getting bad vibes about Tony Bartha and I'm glad I've made up my mind to get rid of him. Well, I won't keep you any longer, dear. Tell Laura again how much we enjoyed her cake."

"I will, Aunt Emily, goodbye."

I sat and thought about my aunt's phone call for a few minutes. Was Tony Bartha selling drugs to kids? And was he putting some kind of pressure on Donald? I was infinitely relieved that Aunt Emily was getting rid of him. He gave off bad vibes in all directions.

I went back to my sewing and worked until Laura announced that dinner was ready. She had been testing German recipes all afternoon and informed me we were having Mittagessin Rouladen—Laura likes using the German names to surprise me. It turned out to be rolled beef with a savory sauce that included red wine and special spices, served with a Bavarian green bean salad. I pronounced it a triumph and Laura looked pleased with her afternoon's work. Mittagessin Rouladen, she told me, would probably be one of the four-star dinners at her Bavarian restaurant.

After dinner, Laura and I slipped on coats and boots and left the apartment. We stood on the sidewalk in front of the

93

building and peered at the trees that lined the lane. There was no sign of anyone here. Feeling brave because there were two of us, we walked the length of the building on the lane side, scrutinizing the trees. No one there. Lieutenant Philippe had taken care of the watcher in the lane. Relieved, but puzzled, we went back to our apartment. Who could it have been and what had he been doing there?

I worked diligently on my dress until eleven and then decided to call it a day. If I got up early tomorrow I could have the dress finished by lunchtime. I had to get it finished by then. Chris and I intended to go to Old Montreal in the afternoon and have dinner later in one of the French restaurants there.

Chapter 13

At nine o'clock Sunday morning I was hard at work on my dress while Laura pounded her ear. Fortunately I've got one of those sleek modern machines that doesn't make much noise, so I didn't have to worry about waking Laura up. She got up about eleven and I stopped sewing long enough to have coffee with her. Then back to the sewing machine. By twelve o'clock the dress was finished except for the hem. I tried it on for length and was delighted by what I saw in the mirror—a tiny-waisted, billowy-skirted dream of a dress —just as I'd pictured it. And the brilliant pink set off my black hair and fair complexion to perfection. Happily I took the dress off and prepared to hem it. I'd just gotten started on it when Laura called me to the phone. It was Chris.

After a little preliminary chitchat about last night's date, Chris got down to the purpose of his call.

"I'm sorry to disappoint you, Nicky, but I won't be able to go this afternoon. I can still make it for dinner, though, if that's okay."

I felt a surge of disappointment and annoyance. We'd planned on spending the afternoon browsing through craft and antique shops before dinner. I was crazy about antiques and had started collecting small pieces with a view to furnishing my future home with them.

"Why can't you go this afternoon, Chris?"

"Because, Muffet, the deadline for my book is February first and I've got to produce so much a day to finish on time. I'd counted on getting today's quota done this morning, but it didn't work out that way. So I've got to work on the book this afternoon and get something written. I know you're disappointed, but I'm too close to the deadline to let days slip by without accomplishing anything. If you're anxious to look at antiques, why don't you go down yourself and I'll meet you for dinner at seven at Chez Pierre."

There it was again. His writing came before a date with me. I felt the tide of annoyance surge into outright anger. A date was a date. Stubbornly, I said, "What difference will a few hours make in the final outcome, Chris? I've been looking forward to this afternoon. You can make up the time another day."

There was an edge of annoyance in Chris's voice now. "I told you, I've got to get so much done a day to make the deadline. And I'm meeting you for dinner. Isn't that good enough?"

Angry that he wouldn't back down, I said sarcastically, "What am I supposed to do between the time the shops close at five and you meet me at seven—walk the streets!"

Now Chris was angry. "Go into Notre Dame Cathedral and pray for my soul, Nicole. And if you change your mind about dinner, call me back."

The receiver clicked softly in my ear. Furious, I strode back to my room and glared at the beautiful dress spread out on the bed. This was the way it would always be. A book would come between me and Chris. A *damned* book! I was angry with Chris and angrier with myself. I knew I was being stubborn and childish, but right now I couldn't seem to help it. I was jealous of Chris's writing—as jealous as though it were a flesh-and-blood woman that was taking him away from me.

I flung myself down on the bed and fingered the filmy folds of the dress. I was going to have a good time while I was in Jamaica. Chris wasn't the only pebble on the beach. And if he was sitting by the phone waiting for me to call back, he was in for a long wait. He could work on his blessed book all night for all I cared.

Dejectedly I got up and decided to have lunch. I wasn't in the mood to hem my dress now. I wasn't in the mood to eat, either, and the toasted cheese sandwich and fruit salad tasted like gall and wormwood. Laura commented at the table that I was awfully quiet and I told her I'd had words with Chris. Tactfully she didn't pursue the subject. For which I was thankful. I knew that if I told Laura the whole story she would tell me I was being unreasonable and I already knew that. I also knew I was being childish and selfish, but now my pride wouldn't let me back down and phone Chris back. I gloomed through the afternoon, doing a few household chores and watching TV for a while. Laura went out at five to have dinner with Claire St.-Germaine and compare notes on recipes, leaving me to sulk by myself. I stared morosely out the living room window, watching big heavy flakes of wet snow drift silently down like puffs of cotton batten.

The room was growing dark and I got up to switch on the lights just as the phone rang. It was Aunt Emily to report that she was sick with the flu and would like to borrow Laura's heating pad to ease her aching back. Both the boys were out, she said, but she expected them any time for dinner. Dinner, said Aunt Emily, would be bacon and beans because she felt too sick to cook anything. She'd send one of the boys over after supper for the heating pad. We were winding up our conversation when Aunt Emily said there was someone at the door—probably one of the boys—and we said goodbye. It was ten after six. In a depressed frame of mind, I went to the kitchen and made myself a hamburger and some coffee. I didn't feel like cooking, either.

It was about eight o'clock when I started to wonder why one of the boys hadn't come over for the heating pad. Surely they'd have finished supper by now. And then I decided on the spur of the moment to take it over myself. Maybe I could forget my woes by trying to cheer Aunt Emily up. I'd call her first and tell her I would bring the heating pad over. I let the phone ring a dozen times, but there was no answer. Maybe she was in the bathroom. I'd try again in ten minutes. When I phoned back, there was still no answer. Well, maybe she was soaking in a hot tub to ease the aches. I waited another half-hour and called again. No answer. I began to feel worried. Why didn't she answer her phone? Surely she wouldn't have gone out feeling as sick as she did. And where were the boys? Something was wrong. With a feeling of growing anxiety, I put on my coat and boots, put the heating pad in a bag and hurried out of the building. Aunt Emily's apartment, at the corner of Winnicott and Côte St. Luc, was about the same distance from my place as Kathleen Windsor's, but in the opposite direction. The main entrance was on Côte St. Luc, but I always used the side door on Winnicott. My aunt's apartment was Number 3 on the main floor.

I was about to knock when I noticed that the door was open a crack. I frowned. Aunt Emily wouldn't have left the door unlocked. Probably one of the boys had left it open after coming in tonight. I pushed the door open and walked in, calling her name so as not to startle her. There was no response. I hesitated a second in the living room, calling louder,

"Aunt Emily, it's Nicky," and walked to the kitchen. I stopped dead at the door. Something was on the floor. The eyes in the bluish-tinged, fear-contorted face seemed to be staring at me. It was Aunt Emily's face. Somehow I knew instantly that she had been murdered. I slumped against the doorframe, my mind drowning in a tidal wave of horror. Slowly the wave receded and the room and reality came back into focus. The eyes were still staring at me with a desperate plea in them. I screamed and screamed again. Then I was running, running on rubbery legs, running out of the nightmare and down the hall, pounding frantically at the first door I came to. It was not real, not real. Not the anxious eyes of a gray-haired woman looking into mine, or the whispered words I heard coming from my own strangled throat: "Aunt Emily . . . Mrs. Teasdale . . . Mrs. Teasdale in Apartment Three—" The eyes were big with alarm; then they blurred and faded into the distance. Then they weren't there any more.

I stared hard at little white flowers on a green background. I stared hard and tried to concentrate. The walls of my room were yellow. I was sure they were yellow. Something cold was on my head and somebody was holding my wrist. I turned my eyes away from the white flowers and looked into the frightened eyes of a gray-haired, matronly woman. Hadn't I seen her before? Consciousness returned with merciless swiftness. Aunt Emily. Aunt Emily was dead.

There were tears in the woman's eyes. "My husband went down to Mrs. Teasdale's apartment. . . . Don't think about it, my dear, whatever you do, don't think about it. My husband has called the police."

I struggled into a sitting position and the wet cloth on my head fell into my lap. The woman removed it. "Bob," she called in a quivery voice, "she's awake now. Bring the brandy."

He appeared from nowhere with a brandy glass in his hands, put an arm around me, held the glass to my lips. He was small and worn-looking and his face was as white as death. Death. I gulped the brandy hungrily, eager to deaden

98

the keen edge of consciousness, to blot out the picture engraved indelibly on my mind—the picture of the face on the kitchen floor. The brandy helped. The image in my mind blurred and a chilling numbness took possession of me. Chris, I thought dully, I have to call Chris. Chris will help. Chris will help me get through it.

The woman was stroking my hand gently. "I'm Mrs. Geoffrey and this is my husband, Bob."

"How do you do," I said formally. I wasn't sure that they were real or that the room was real. "Could you call someone for me?"

"Of course, my dear." The man named Bob produced a pad of paper and pencil and wrote down Chris's number. Before he went away to phone he gave me another drink of brandy. I drank it greedily. The numbness in my head spread to my body. My hand was limp in the hand of Mrs. Geoffrey.

"A terrible, terrible thing," she quavered, as though I didn't know. "Mrs. Teasdale was such a nice little person. And your aunt . . . how awful for you. But don't think about it, my dear. It doesn't bear thinking of. Your friend will be here soon." She was holding on to self-control with a supreme effort of will.

I tried to picture Aunt Emily as I'd seen her last summer on her motorcycle, the frail little body quivering with aliveness, the squirrel-bright black eyes sparkling with enjoyment. But I couldn't hold it long. Someone kept changing the slide. Someone kept changing it to the slide of the kitchen floor.

There was a whispered consultation at the door leading to the hall. Mr. Geoffrey was squeezing Mrs. Geoffrey's hand. Then the door buzzer sounded, far away as though there was an invisible wall between me and the world outside my numb mind and body. Dimly I heard masculine voices in the hall, footsteps receding, a door closing. The door opened again a few minutes later, the voices came back. I heard the faint dialing of a phone, a low-voiced conversation. Then two big policemen were standing in front of me. One of them was holding a notebook and pen. Mrs. Geoffrey sat down beside me.

"They have to ask some questions, my dear, but I told them not to ask any more than is absolutely necessary right now."

The dark-haired one—he looked too young to be a policeman—addressed me in a heavily accented voice, his tone apologetic.

"I will only ask a few questions, mademoiselle. Detectives from Homicide will be down shortly and they will go into more detail with you. Mrs. Teasdale was your aunt?"

"Yes," I answered woodenly, "Mrs. Teasdale was my aunt."

Obediently I answered questions put to me, watching the sandy-haired constable's hand as he scribbled away on the pad. There were curly golden hairs on the fingers and I gave them the same intense concentration I had given the white flowers on the green wallpaper when my mind had first stirred back to consciousness. If I concentrated hard enough on those busily moving fingers maybe the picture in my mind would dissolve—the picture of Aunt Emily's bluish-tinged face on the kitchen floor. How cruel, how savagely, monstrously cruel.

The questions stopped suddenly. "That is all, mademoiselle," said the one who looked too young to be a policeman. "We must wait for—"

The door buzzer pealed far away and he left me abruptly. There were voices in the hall again and then the black-haired constable was back.

"The men from Homicide are here. They have gone to— It will not be long, mademoiselle."

I didn't say anything. They had gone to look. I didn't like the idea of strangers looking at Aunt Emily like that. There would be a photographer, wouldn't there? Taking pictures? And somebody for fingerprints, and a doctor? I wanted to protest. They shouldn't be in there looking at Aunt Emily,

100

touching her. I wanted to object, but I couldn't. Of what use to protest final indignities? Of what use to protest anything now? Aunt Emily was dead.

The next time the door buzzer sounded it was Chris. Mrs. Geoffrey led him in, his face white, jaw set in a grim line. Was it just a few hours ago we had quarreled? But that was in another world. In a few strides he was beside me, holding me hard against the hardness of his chest.

"I'll get you out of here as soon as I can, Muffet. Try and hold together. Lisa is going to stay with you tonight. You'll feel better with Lisa there."

I let the deep, compassionate voice flow through me, warming the edges of the numbness, thawing a little the frozen edges of my mind. It was enough that Chris was there.

The door buzzer rang again and the two constables left the room. Mr. and Mrs. Geoffrey sat on a love seat across from me. Mr. Geoffrey was patting his wife's shoulder. When the two policemen returned they had company. A tall, hawk-faced individual and a smaller, weary-looking man wearing a battered felt hat.

Lieutenant Philippe doffed his hat and bowed slightly. The gray eyes were as bleak as death, but the voice was gentle. "I am sorry, mademoiselle," he said simply. "We will not detain you any longer than necessary."

He conferred with the dark-haired young constable, read the notes of the sandy-haired one, with the hawk-faced man reading along beside him. Then they turned to me. Chris spoke first, his arm protectively around me.

"Please make it as quick as possible. She's in no state to be questioned."

The hawk-faced one gave Chris a searching look from piercing black eyes. Then he turned to me. "I'm Lieutenant Beaubien, mademoiselle. Just a few questions about those boys that were staying with your aunt. Tomorrow, when you have . . . have recovered from the shock, we will want to talk to you again. You told the constable someone came to your

101

aunt's door when you were talking to her on the phone and she thought it was the boys. Will you please tell me what you can of these boys?"

I told Lieutenant Beaubien what I could of the drop-in center and Aunt Emily bringing the two boys home. I told him my aunt had intended to keep Donald Hammill until a home was found for him by the authorities but that she meant to ask Tony Bartha to leave. The lieutenant of course wanted to know why Aunt Emily had intended to get rid of Tony. I told the detective about my aunt's suspicions of Tony and he listened hard, while the sandy-haired constable's blunt fingers again flew across a pad of paper. Lieutenant Philippe slouched in a chair in front of me, looking morosely at the battered hat in his lap.

"And what was Bartha's reaction when your aunt asked him to leave?"

"I don't know. That is, I don't know if she told him. I talked to her yesterday afternoon and she said she was going to speak to Tony. When I talked to her today she didn't mention it."

"So you don't know whether your aunt told Bartha to leave or not. And she was expecting both boys for dinner? What exactly did she say when her buzzer sounded when you were on the phone?"

"She said that must be the boys, and then we said good-bye."

"And what time was this, mademoiselle?"

"It was ten after six. I looked at my watch just after I hung up."

"Will you describe these boys as accurately as you can?"

"Donald was tall and gangly. Wheat blond hair, corn-flower blue eyes. He played the guitar. Wore jeans and a black pullover when I saw him. Tony was pale, with shifty-looking eyes and greasy black hair of medium length. And he was small and undernourished-looking."

"How small, mademoiselle?"

I couldn't seem to think clearly. And I was so tired of the

102

questions. "I couldn't say exactly—maybe five feet five, and thin."

Lieutenant Beaubien looked at me hard. "Do you think he was strong enough to strangle your aunt?"

I gasped. "She was . . . was *strangled?*"

The hunter's eyes softened a little. "The doctor thinks so, but he cannot say for sure until an autopsy is performed. There are no more questions for now. We will be in touch with you again."

I got up shakily. Chris put a steadying hand on my arm. Mr. and Mrs. Geoffrey shook hands with me.

"I hope they get him, Miss Nugent. I'll pray that they get him," Mr. Geoffrey said earnestly.

At the door, Lieutenant Philippe patted my arm awkwardly. There was pity in the cynical gray eyes. "We will do everything we can to apprehend the killer, mademoiselle."

We all filed out silently. In five minutes Chris and I were home and he was taking off my coat, guiding me to a sofa in the bright yellow and green living room. I sat silently, woodenly, my weighted brain trying to grasp the incredible, monstrous fact. Aunt Emily was dead. Strangled. Chris busied himself making a fire, glancing at me from time to time with worried eyes. The fire was what we needed. Bright searing flames to keep at bay the evil that stalked the night.

Lisa and Guy arrived half an hour later, Guy, for once, subdued and solemn-faced. Beautiful, serene Lisa's eyes were wet. She took me in her Earth Mother's arms and rocked me gently. She wanted me to cry, but I couldn't. I was dead. I heard them talking faint and far away through the cocoon that enveloped me, soft and weightless as snowflakes.

"I brought some sleeping pills, Chris. I'm going to put her to sleep. Don't worry. Tomorrow she'll be better."

Lisa brought a bright red pill and a glass of water to me. I swallowed obediently. I hoped it didn't take long to take effect. It would be good to sleep. Then Lisa was guiding me down the hall to my room, talking to me gently. She put out a nightgown for me, turned down the covers of my bed and tucked me in. She sat beside me while the room fogged and blurred. Rising from the fog was a face—a discolored, fear-contorted face. Then the fog rolled over the face and there was only blackness.

Chapter 14

Monday's skyscape was gray, heavy, with sweeps of angry black cloud that presaged storm. The heavens were protesting the slaughter of the innocent, I thought dully as I closed the window against the raw damp, shivering in my thin housecoat. My head was heavy, fuzzy, and my heart was as leaden as the skies. Moving like a robot, I washed, brushed my hair, carefully chose a navy blue wool from my cupboard, added a double strand of pearls. That would be suitable, wouldn't it? Suitable for talking to detectives, making arrangements with a funeral home, greeting Aunt Emily's other relatives? Not today the gray flannel pants and bright red sweater. Today was different. Today Aunt Emily was dead.

I was surprised to meet Lisa in the hall. Then I remembered. Chris had said she would stay with me. Wordlessly she put an arm around me, led me to the kitchen, steered me to a chair.

"You'll feel better after you've eaten something, Nicky. Then we'll talk. Laura said since I was staying here today she'd go to work; then she can take the day of the funeral off to help out. Chris will be down at ten."

I watched Lisa's hands as she poured orange juice, flipped

104

an egg onto a plate. Beautiful hands that would soon caress a baby. A new life to replace the one so brutally snuffed out. Lisa poured coffee, brought everything to the table. I shouldn't be just sitting here. I should be doing something. There was so much to be done. "Lisa, we've got to notify Aunt Emily's relatives. There's Uncle Harold in Kingston and Aunt—"

"Eat first, Nicky, eat everything. Then we'll tackle things one at a time." Lisa's rich, husky voice was firm.

I made myself eat. I had to swallow hard to make the toast go down. But I felt better after I'd finished. The coffee cleared the fuzz from my head. Now I could think clearly.

"I have to call the school, Lisa, tell them—"

"Laura called for you before she left for work. Miss Eden was dreadfully sorry. She said if there was anything they could do for you—no matter how small—to let her know. And Chris got your Uncle Harold's address from Lieutenant Beaubien. He found it on your aunt's telephone list. Chris called Mr. Craig last night. Your uncle said he would notify everybody else in the family and he was putting a death notice in the paper with instructions for Montreal papers to copy. He said he would phone this morning. I think we'd better wait until—"

The phone shrilled and Lisa went to answer it. There was a low-voiced conversation in the hall and then she was back.

"It's your Uncle Harold. Do you feel like talking to him?"

"Yes, I'll take it, Lisa."

Uncle Harold's voice sounded old, broken. "Nicky, baby, it's a terrible, terrible thing and I'm so sorry you had to find her like that. So sorry. Are you all right, baby?"

"I'm all right, Uncle Harold."

"I talked to May last night. Between us, we've seen to it that everyone's been notified. Emily had a plot next to her husband in the Pines cemetery, so the funeral will be in Montreal. Your Aunt May's taking the four-twenty plane from Toronto today. I'm leaving here at noon. Should be there about three. Helen will be with me. Just one thing. Can you arrange hotel

105

accommodations for us? There'll be Helen and I, and May and Allan for tonight and tomorrow night. So we need two rooms. And another two for tomorrow night, when May's two boys and Anna and Ken will be down. There may be others coming, but we can take care of that later. For now, two rooms for tonight and tomorrow, and another two rooms for tomorrow night. Can you look after that, baby?"

I was making notes on a pad. "I'll look after it. But what about Aunt Emily . . . I mean . . . the . . . the body? Where do you want it sent?"

"Oh, I'd completely forgotten. . . . Do you know the name of a good funeral home in Montreal, Nicky?"

"Harrison's. Harrison's is very good."

"Then we'll make it Harrison's. When will the body be released? Did they tell you?"

"No, Uncle Harold, but I can find out. I'll find out and instruct them to send it to Harrison's. Is that what you want?"

"Yes, yes," said the old, broken voice. "If you can manage it, baby, and we'll take care of everything else when we get there. We'll phone you when we arrive in Montreal to see where you've booked rooms. Then we'll check in and leave our baggage before going to your place."

"All right. We'll expect to hear from you around three."

Lisa was standing beside me when I hung up. "I'll make the arrangements about the body, Nicky, and the hotel reservations for your relatives. There'll be a lot more phone calls to be made, but some things will have to wait until your uncle gets here and tells you what he wants done. Maybe you could make a list of the people your aunt knows in Montreal who should be notified."

"I don't really know, aside from her church choir. She knew so many people, but all I ever heard was first names. Oh . . . the obituary notice . . . a lot of people will probably learn about it from the obituary notice. I wonder if it will make today's paper."

"It will if your uncle called it in last night. Chris will be

106

here soon. Why don't you just sit and try to relax until he gets here?"

But I couldn't sit and relax. I had to do something, anything. I went to work on the breakfast dishes. I was rubbing ferociously at a hardened egg blob on a plate when Chris walked in. I'd thrown myself into the task so single-mindedly I hadn't heard the buzzer sound. He squeezed me gently, then tilted my head up, looked at me intently.

"How are you, Muffet?"

"I'm all right, Chris. It's just that it . . . it takes a little time. Nothing seems real somehow."

"I know, dear, I know. Don't try to rush it. Just ride with it. It will get easier after a while. I just wish to God it hadn't been you who found her. Those detectives we saw last night . . . they want to talk to you again today. Philippe told me they didn't go through the whole drill with you last night. They thought you were too stunned to think clearly. Do you think you could take it today, Nicky?"

"Yes, I can take it." I could take almost anything if it led to the finding of my aunt's murderer. "Do you think they could come down before three? Aunt Emily's brother and his wife are coming at three."

"They wanted to talk to you as soon as possible. I'll ask them if they can come down this morning."

Chris reported a few minutes later that Lieutenants Beaubien and Philippe would be down in half an hour. It had been Lieutenant Beaubien who had asked all the questions last night. "Is he in charge of the case?" I wondered aloud.

"No, Nicky, Beaubien is a fledgling detective who's learning the ropes from Philippe. Philippe is in charge of the Windsor murder case and your aunt's. Because there is such a similarity between the two murders, Philippe volunteered to work on both. Two other men are working on the Grunberger murder. They are all working individually but teaming up to compare notes."

Lisa was still busy on the phone when Lieutenants Philippe

and Beaubien arrived, with a uniformed constable trailing behind them. Chris led them into the living room, where I was senselessly dusting a gleaming table top. Lieutenant Philippe, rubbing the pouch under his left eye, looked as though he'd been up all night. It turned out they had both been up all night.

Lieutenant Philippe bowed slightly, his battered hat clutched to his chest. It was the craggy-faced one who spoke.

"Mademoiselle, we know you are tired and under strain. We too are tired and under strain. We have had two hours' sleep after an all-night conference on the recent strangling murders in the area. There must be no more. I ask your fullest co-operation. The questions I ask are important. Please answer as clearly and completely as you can. No question I ask is irrelevant, although it may seem so. We will begin with the obvious. Your aunt had two boys staying with her. Both boys have disappeared. We left a man in Mrs. Teasdale's apartment last night. Neither boy returned. Some of their belongings are still there. Will you tell me again everything you know about those two boys?"

Tony Bartha, I thought, Tony Bartha with the surly face and the shifty eyes. Had Aunt Emily told him to leave? Had Tony in a rage—?

"Mlle. Nugent?"

I started. "I'm sorry, Lieutenant." And then I told him everything I could about Tony Bartha and Donald Hammill —everything Aunt Emily had told me—the impressions I'd gathered from their visit to my place on Friday night. I came to a stop.

Chris sat on one side of me. The auburn-haired constable with his notebook and pen on the other. The detectives sat facing us, on chairs drawn up to the sofa. I kept my eyes on the constable's busy hands. I didn't want to look into the black eyes watching me—the eyes of a hunter. Lieutenant Beaubien was talking to me again.

"Do you think either boy was capable of murder?"

Tony Bartha? If he was selling drugs to public school children, maybe anything was possible. I really didn't know. I thought of those nervously drumming fingers. But he was too small. But Aunt Emily was smaller. Aunt Emily was tiny. And Donald? I saw Donald's big hands caressing music from his guitar. Could those hands have—?

"Mlle. Nugent?"

I came out of my reverie, apologized again for my mind-wandering. I answered the question as best I could. And the questions that came after. There seemed to be a hundred, and some of them didn't make much sense, but I answered them obediently. Now and then Chris squeezed my hand encouragingly. When I glanced at Lieutenant Philippe, the bitter gray eyes softened, sent a message of sympathy. He sagged in his chair as though too exhausted to sit up, his sad, bloodhound face more melancholy than ever.

The questions went on and on: What did I know of Aunt Emily's friends? Did she have any men friends? Was she in the habit of leaving her door unlocked? Did she keep large sums of money in the house? Did I know any of the people in her church choir. What names had she mentioned? Think, Miss Nugent, Think. It's very important. He wanted names, names of people at her church. But I couldn't think of any besides Kathleen Windsor and Elsie Grunberger. And then I realized why Lieutenant Beaubien was so insistent about the church. The three victims had all been members of St. Simon's choir. Coincidence? *Three* of them? I tried harder to remember, but the only names I could recall Aunt Emily having mentioned were Kathleen Windsor and Elsie Grunberger. And the choir director. But I couldn't recall the name. It was all right, said Lieutenant Beaubien, they could easily check that. And then, suddenly, the questions came to an end. The auburn-haired constable stopped scribbling and closed his notebook.

Now it was my turn. I had a question I was almost afraid to ask. I couldn't bear it if the answer was yes. But I had to know.

I addressed Lieutenant Philippe. I was a little afraid of the hawk-faced one.

"Lieutenant Philippe, was my aunt—sexually molested?"

"No, mademoiselle, she was spared that indignity. But as in the case of the Grunberger woman, it may have been that the killer did not have time. Your aunt was expecting the boys any minute. They may have rung the doorbell even as the killer was in the apartment. He could have then escaped by the side entrance on Winnicott without being seen by the boys."

"Then you don't think it was one of the boys?"

Lieutenant Philippe sighed wearily. "We don't know. We must consider every possibility. But we are inclined to think that one man is responsible for all three strangling murders. And the fact that all three women belonged to St. Simon's choir gives us strong reason to suppose the killer is a member of St. Simon's Church. Lieutenant Beaubien and I are questioning the choir members again tonight. We've got to find a lead fast—before there are any more murders."

The trio of policemen stood up and Chris and I followed their lead. At the door, Lieutenant Philippe turned to me.

"You are not a member of St. Simon's choir?"

"No," I said, gasping at the implication of the question.

"Nevertheless, be careful, mademoiselle." Then they were gone.

While we had been talking to the police, Lisa had prepared lunch for us. We ate silently, without enthusiasm. It was over coffee that Chris spoke directly of the murder, broke the spell of unreality that seemed to hold us all in thrall. His eyes were icy blue with anger.

"You'd think with all those men working on it, they'd get somewhere. But they seem to be running around like rats in a maze. Every turning they take is the wrong one. And in the meantime, a psychopath is running around loose."

"You think it *is* a psychopath, Chris?"

"Three women murdered within a block of each other in

a two-week period. What other explanation is there? And they sit wasting time asking questions about Donald and Tony."

"But," I said doubtfully, "they both disappeared. It does look bad. And if Aunt Emily told Tony she wanted him to leave, then he would have had a grudge against her. But even if it was Tony, I can't understand Donald disappearing."

"It's likely they went back to your aunt's apartment last night, found her murdered and panicked. If Tony was mixed up in drug dealing, he had reason to be afraid of the police. And Donald was a babe in the woods. If Tony panicked, Donald would have too. Probably the only thought in their heads was to put as much space between them and your aunt's apartment as possible." Chris frowned, ran his hand through his springy brown hair. "Whoever came to your aunt's apartment last night when you were talking to her on the phone *must* have been the killer."

Lisa spoke quietly. "Is there a peephole in your aunt's door, Nicky."

"Yes, there is."

"Then she could see who was at the door. Would she open the door to a stranger?"

"I don't know," I said slowly. Aunt Emily had been trusting, but she had not been a fool. Still, I'd found her door open when I'd gone there last night. But that didn't mean it had been open when the killer had come calling.

Chris's square, ruddy face was thoughtful. "You know, I didn't go along with your Lieutenant Philippe's theory that Kathleen Windsor had opened her door at midnight to her murderer because she knew him. But now I'm beginning to wonder. All three women were members of St. Simon's choir. If it is somebody at the church, it begins to make sense. In that case Kathleen Windsor and Aunt Emily would have opened the door because they knew the man and thought they had nothing to fear from him." He pushed his chair away from the table, got up. "Talking about it won't solve anything.

Would you like to go for a walk, Nicky, to get some fresh air before your aunt and uncle arrive?"

Lisa looked at me. "Go ahead, Nicky, I'll take care of the dishes."

For nearly an hour Chris and I walked hand in hand down familiar streets, our footsteps muffled by thick falling snow. The feeling of unreality still had a grip on me and it was strange to see cars moving up and down, people walking along with parcels, talking in twos at street corners. Strange to see life going on as usual when the world had stopped for me.

On our way back to the apartment we stopped at a tobacco shop and bought a paper. I didn't want to see if there was anything about my aunt's murder in the paper. I didn't want to hear any more about it. I just wanted to see if the death notice was in.

When we got home just before three Lisa told us my aunt and uncle were on their way down. They arrived half an hour later, Uncle Harold, who is fifty-eight, looking suddenly old and stooped, his face ravaged by grief. His wife, a calm, practical woman, wore a dazed expression on her pleasant middle-aged face.

Uncle Harold hugged me wordlessly, his eyes suspiciously bright. Aunt Helen squeezed my hand hard. She was not, normally, a demonstrative woman.

I served sherry to everyone and then we got down to the painful business of planning Aunt Emily's funeral. After two hours' discussion and a dozen phone calls, everything was arranged. The funeral would be on Wednesday at ten o'clock from St. Simon's Church. St. Simon's choir would sing at the service and the Reverend George Henley would conduct the short service at the graveside. I would assist Uncle Harold and his wife and Aunt May and her husband in receiving visitors at Harrison's funeral home tomorrow. Flowers were ordered, pallbearers decided on. After the funeral there would be a reception for mourners at my place. Laura had said she would

112

take the day of the funeral off and I knew she would help with a luncheon. Lisa came into the room while we were discussing the luncheon and told me that she and Laura would take charge of that chore and leave me free to circulate among the mourners.

Guy picked Lisa up at five-thirty and she offered to come down again on Tuesday, but I told her it wasn't necessary. We said goodbye at the door, Lisa promising to be at the apartment at nine on Wednesday morning. I thought Guy seemed a little surly. I had the feeling he didn't like having Lisa's attention diverted from himself for even a day or two.

Chris left a few minutes later and then Aunt May phoned to announce her arrival in Montreal. Laura came home from work while they were on the phone. Her gamin face was a study in sadness and her eyes were red. "I'm so sorry, Nicky, so terribly sorry. Your aunt was such a pet . . . how could anyone—" Her voice broke, then she regained control. "I'm not going to school tonight. I'm going to get dinner for everyone and do the dishes so you can have your time free for your aunt and uncle. I'll use my room tonight and you can have the living room to yourself."

The four of us ate at the long table in front of the big windows in the living room. Wind-driven snow whirled about outside in the darkness as though spewn from the mouth of a snow blower. I'd made up a good fire and the heat of the flames warmed the numbness in my body a little. But not my heart. My heart was frozen with grief and rage. Between bites of food, Uncle Harold kept up a steady stream of reminiscences about Aunt Emily. He talked about their youth and their early adult years before Aunt Emily moved to Montreal. He talked about her monthly visits to Kingston and the summer holidays she spent at their cottage near Barrys Bay in Ontario. And through it all, ran the thread of her warmth and aliveness, her insatiable curiosity about people, her all-embracing zest for life.

All of us recognized that Uncle Harold needed to talk

113

about his sister—that the flow of speech was like a healing balm on the gaping wound he had sustained with her murder. We listened silently, nodding now and then, asking a pertinent question, careful not to break the thread of his narrative. Finally Uncle Harold petered out, drank his coffee in silence, his kindly face etched in lines of grief.

Aunt May and Uncle Allan arrived at eight. Their faces mirrored their shock and sorrow. Hands were shaken, kisses exchanged. In hushed voices they expressed their outrage and grief. I left the two of them in the living room with Uncle Harold and Aunt Helen and went to help Laura with the dishes.

There seemed to be a lot of telephone calls and Laura took them all. And twice the door buzzer pealed. The first time it was the pastor of St. Simon's Church come to offer his condolences in person. The second time it was the choir director of St. Simon's to confer on the hymns to be sung at the funeral service. Mrs. Anderson was sorry to arrive so late, but she had just come from a conference at the church with the police. All the members of the choir had been contacted by phone in the afternoon and every single member had turned up tonight to offer their fullest co-operation to the police. Mrs. Teasdale, the director said in her throaty voice, would be sadly missed by the choir and they all prayed that her slayer would be swiftly brought to justice. Yes, I thought dully, I was sure they were all praying that her killer would be caught, because who knew who might be the next victim? The Reverend George Henley offered to drive Mrs. Anderson home and she accepted with great alacrity. And who could blame her? I wasn't going anywhere alone myself these nights if I could help it.

The aunts and uncles left at eleven. We would meet again at Harrison's funeral home tomorrow at 10 A.M. I felt drained, exhausted. I wanted to sleep and sleep, but I was afraid to go to bed. Afraid of what scenes my mind's eye would conjure up when I lay quietly in the dark with my eyes closed. The

114

sleeping pill Lisa had given me last night had been good . . .
I wished I'd asked her . . . but maybe Laura . . . There was
a knock at the bathroom door. I opened it to Laura.

"I was going to ask you if you wanted to talk awhile, but
you look beat. You'd better go to bed. Lisa left some sleeping
pills for you in the medicine cabinet. She thought you might
need them for a week or so."

I sighed with relief. Lisa thought of everything. Now I
could go swiftly, mercifully to sleep—without thinking. I
couldn't bear to think yet.

Chapter 15

I spent most of Tuesday at the funeral home with my aunts
and uncles. Three nieces and two nephews of Aunt Emily's
arrived in the morning and with so many assisting in the task
of receiving visitors, we were able to take frequent short breaks
in pairs. It was a relief to get away from the funeral home
with its somber, hushed atmosphere, the air heavy with the
scent of flowers, heavy with the finality of death. A ten-minute
walk around the block, a cup of coffee in a nearby restaurant,
and we were ready to go back: to shake more hands, listen
to more condolences, comfort and be comforted.

A bewildering variety of people came to pay their last
respects to Emily Teasdale. It seemed she had known all
the "little" people in Montreal. There was the grizzled shoemaker who said Aunt Emily had been a woman after his own
heart. She had demanded that stout thick soles be put on her
shoes, none of those fashionable skinny soles that wore out in
no time: shoes were for walking, weren't they? And she

115

wanted cleats on her heels—so people could hear her coming. Otherwise they might miss her entirely, she being so small, she had told the shoemaker. And there was the little cleaning woman who worked at the Montreal General. She and Mrs. Teasdale had had some rare old talks when Mrs. Teasdale had been a patient for a month last year. Mrs. Teasdale had got so many flowers and every morning she'd present the cleaning lady with the most beautiful flower in the newest bunch she'd received. And she'd gone hopping about the wards doing little services for those who were bedridden. As Mrs. Teasdale put it, she couldn't just lie abed doing nothing while she had two good legs to move about on. There was the tea importer on Bleury where Aunt Emily had gone every month for her special blend of Darjeeling tea. Mrs. Teasdale had known almost as much about tea as he did, he said. There were a dozen young Krishna monks in saffron-colored robes with tilaks painted on their foreheads, a supermarket clerk, the members of her choir, a gang of long-haired youth of both sexes from the drop-in center, old friends from Toronto. They had all admired the generous spirit of the fragile little woman who had been taken from their midst—so violently, so senselessly.

At five o'clock my two aunts and uncles went back to their hotel for a short rest and dinner. At seven Chris came down and took me to dinner at a small, quiet restaurant on Decarie. Then I went back to Harrison's—back to the flower-banked room, the flickering tapers, the mahogany casket where Aunt Emily rested—eyes sealed forever against the world of maya.

I read the cards on the floral offerings—sprays, wreaths, tiny bouquets. There was a spray of pink carnations from Julian Brooks. He came with Laura at nine o'clock, his vulnerable, boyish face solemn.

"I'm so frightfully sorry, Nicky. Your aunt was such an alive person. I can hardly believe— I hope they get him," he finished in a whisper, his jaw set in a hard line.

Laura and Julian stayed there until I was ready to leave at

116

ten. Julian drove us home but didn't come in. I heard him telling Laura he would see her on Friday. When we got in Laura told me she had done some of the preliminary work on tomorrow's luncheon and with Lisa coming early in the morning, they'd have everything ready by noon. They didn't know how many to expect but were preparing for a big crowd. Uncle Harold had arranged for the cars to take the mourners to the church. I would be going with Chris. He was calling for me at nine. There didn't seem to be anything else that needed looking after tonight.

Thankfully I slipped out of my clothes and put on my nightgown. Laura and I talked a few minutes; then I went to bed. Tomorrow it would be all over and things would be normal again. But how could things be normal again after someone you loved had been murdered?

Chapter 16

"'Eternal rest grant unto her, O Lord . . .'" The Reverend George Henley's voice rang out in the cold, crisp air. A bright sun struck light off the bronze handles of the casket, its austere form softened by floral wreaths and sprays. Now and then a muffled sob dimmed the minister's voice. Then the short service at the graveside was over and the mourners turned away, dabbing furtively at eyes with handkerchiefs. I glanced back once to bid a silent last farewell to Aunt Emily. Then I hurried away, away from the flower-decked casket, the barren trees, the snow-covered ground of the cemetery. Aunt May, beside me, was weeping openly. Chris and I, with two of my cousins, rode back to Phoebe Lane in silence.

117

Within half an hour the apartment was overflowing with people, people of every age and description—many of them red-eyed from weeping. Lisa and Laura had set up a buffet luncheon on the long refectory table in the living room, and at Laura's big desk by the windows a strange woman presided over silver coffee and tea urns. Later in the afternoon, Laura introduced me to her. It was Claire St.-Germaine, the woman who was going into the restaurant business with Laura. When she had heard of Aunt Emily's death and the preparations for a reception for the mourners, she'd offered to come and help and Laura had eagerly taken her up on it. And with that crowd, Laura and Lisa needed all the help they could get.

I moved from group to group, introducing myself, shaking hands, listening to now familiar expressions of grief and outrage. The members of St. Simon's choir huddled together by the windows, as though they thought there was safety in numbers. The third murder among their members had left them all shocked, wide-eyed with an unspoken fear. Mrs. Anderson, the choir director, hovered around the fringes of the group, as though trying to protect them all at once.

When the crowd thinned out a little I took a quick break for a sandwich and coffee in the kitchen. I was drinking my coffee when a small, ascetic-looking man with a red beard walked in and approached me diffidently. He was carrying a brown, squarish-looking package under one arm.

"I wonder if you could tell me who is the closest kin to Mrs. Teasdale here?"

"That would be her brother and sister, Harold Craig and May Adams. Would you like to talk to them?"

He spoke very quietly and his eyes were a soft puzzled brown. "I'd like to talk to Mr. Craig, if I may. Could you bring him in here where it's quiet? I want to show him something."

"Yes, wait here and I'll get him." I found Uncle Harold saying goodbye to someone at the door and brought him back to the kitchen with me. The red-bearded man acknowledged the introduction solemnly and started to untie the string on the brown package.

"I met Mrs. Teasdale last summer at Dominion Square Park. I was trying to sell my paintings there and Mrs. Teasdale used to sit and chat with me by the hour. I wasn't doing very well and was discouraged. She'd pump me full of enthusiasm for my work and then I'd decide to stick it out a little longer. She was always so eager to see my newest work. She'd hop from painting to painting like a little cock sparrow, head tilted on one side, bright black eyes taking in everything. Mrs. Teasdale believed in me—so I started to believe in myself. Now several small art galleries are showing my work."

His long, sensitive fingers were stripping the parcel from its wrapping. Then he held it up. It was a portrait of Aunt Emily, done in oils.

"I managed to get her to keep still long enough to paint her. After the painting sessions were over, Mrs. Teasdale would go off to feed the squirrels and birds." The soft brown eyes looked earnestly at Uncle Harold. "I thought perhaps you'd like to have it."

It was Aunt Emily to the life, seated on a bed of grass, a long cape flowing around her. The artist had caught to perfection the quivering aliveness of the small pointed face, the sharp intelligence in the shining black eyes.

The red-bearded man handed the picture to Uncle Harold and he took it reverently.

"It's so very like her . . . so very like her. I'd be very pleased to have it. It was so kind of you to—" Uncle Harold's voice broke.

"I wanted someone who loved her to have it. Why would anyone want to kill Mrs. Teasdale?" The soft brown eyes looked more puzzled than ever. Then the artist gently patted Uncle Harold's arm and walked out of the kitchen.

"It's a lovely picture of her, Nicky. I'd like to keep it . . . but your Aunt May might like to have it—"

"You can decide on it later, Uncle Harold. I'll put it away

119

in my room for now." I put the painting away and returned to the visitors. By three-thirty the apartment had almost emptied. Laura, Lisa and Claire St.-Germaine tackled the mountain of dishes, Chris and Guy went for a walk and I talked to my aunts and uncles in the living room.

Uncle Harold looked at Aunt May. "I suppose we should go over to Emily's apartment and see about her things. We have to go home tomorrow."

Aunt May's pleasant face looked very tired. "Yes, I think we should go now, Harold, and get it over with. Is there anything of Emily's you'd like to have, Nicky. Anything at all. We'll sell most of her furniture so you may as well have what you want."

"I'd love the pine armoire in Aunt Emily's bedroom. It's a real antique. But I think that's about all." I was praying that Uncle Harold and Aunt May wouldn't ask me to go to the apartment with them. I never wanted to set foot in that place again. And then I thought of Aunt Emily's red motorcycle. Donald Hammill would have loved that motorcycle. But Donald had disappeared. Still, he might come back.

"Aunt Emily had a motorcycle. It's in the garage of her building. That boy Donald she had staying with her—she was very fond of him. I have a feeling she'd like Donald to have that motorcycle."

Uncle Harold frowned. "But Nicky, baby, that boy ran away, he might even have—"

"He didn't kill her," I said quietly. "I'd stake my life on that. Tony, maybe, but not Donald. He thought Aunt Emily was the greatest. And somehow I think he might come back. Of course if you want to sell the motorcycle, you'd probably get a good price for it."

Uncle Harold looked at his sister. "What do you think, May? If this boy really cared about Emily, it would be kind of nice to let him have the motorcycle. We could leave it with Nicky for a few months. Then if he didn't show up, we could see about selling it."

120

Aunt May brushed a strand of gray hair back from her forehead. "I think Emily would like it if we gave her motorcycle to the boy if he comes back. Could you store it here, Nicky?"

"Yes, I can put it in the basement."

Uncle Allan got up decisively. "The four of us will go to Emily's apartment. It will be easier with a group. And then I suggest we all go back to the hotel for dinner. Nicky and her friends must be tired. We must thank them all for the use of the apartment and for the lovely luncheon they prepared."

There were murmurs of assent from the rest of the group and then they all trooped out to the kitchen to thank Laura and Lisa and Claire.

Finally they were ready to leave. Numb, emptied of all emotion, I scarcely heard the farewell conversations at the door. The only words that remained fixed in my mind as the door closed on my uncles and aunts were Uncle Harold's parting sentences.

"Take care of yourself, and baby, please be careful, won't you? You've got to be careful when there's a maniac roaming the neighborhood."

Guy and Chris returned from their walk a few minutes later and Guy headed for the kitchen to claim his wife. He made an ostentatious show of helping Lisa on with her new mink coat, caressing the shimmering fur sensuously before draping it around her shoulders. He smiled affably at Chris.

"And when will the successful novelist be able to buy a beauty like that for his girl?"

There it was—the poisoned arrow. Chris regarded Guy with steady blue eyes and smiled pleasantly. But he didn't say anything. Hastily I started thanking Lisa for all her help. I told her I didn't know how we'd have managed without her and Laura and Claire St.-Germaine. Lisa brushed off my thanks in her serene, gracious manner and then she and Guy left. Chris regarded me thoughtfully.

"You must be tired, Nicky. Would you like me to go home

now so you can rest? Or would you rather I stayed for a while?"

I was tired, so very tired, but I felt I couldn't rest. I wanted Chris's comforting presence here a little longer. I wanted to buy a little time. Just a little more time before I was alone with my thoughts and had to come to grips with the stark reality of Aunt Emily's murder. "I'd like you to stay if you will, Chris. There's food left over from the luncheon, so we won't have to cook anything. But maybe I'd better check first with Laura. She's had the apartment full of strangers for two days now. She might like to have the place to herself for a change."

As it turned out, Laura was glad to hear Chris wanted to stay with me. Claire had asked her to go to dinner at her place and Laura wanted to get away from the apartment but didn't want to leave me alone.

Laura and Claire left half an hour later and Chris and I had the place to ourselves. He got a fire going in the living room while I fixed drinks for us. We sat on the floor by the fireplace and sipped our drinks in silence. It was heavenly to have the apartment free of people, free of talk of Aunt Emily. The air felt heavy and oppressive, as though the atmosphere had retained all those hushed conversations about murder. But the bright flickering tongues of fire would purify the air, cleanse it of the taint of death that hung over the room.

Suddenly I wanted to get away from the apartment, just for a little while. Away from the rooms that had been full of mourners a few hours ago, away from the rooms that held too many memories of Aunt Emily. I glanced at my watch. It was twenty after six.

"Chris, I'd like to go out for a while. Why don't we pack up some food and take it to your place to eat?"

He looked at me and nodded slowly. "I know how you feel, Nicky. I should have thought of it first."

"Finish your drink, Chris. I'll get the food packed."

It was while I was wrapping cold cuts in aluminum foil that I remembered my trip to Jamaica. It was the first time I had

122

thought of it since Aunt Emily's murder. My vacation was just three days away. It would be a relief to get away. Maybe on a palm-fringed shore in the blue Caribbean I could forget these last few days in Montreal, forget the picture of Aunt Emily's frail body on the kitchen floor of her apartment. But I wondered how Laura was going to feel about me going away now. Would she be afraid alone in the apartment after three murders in the area in two weeks? I had to admit that I didn't want to stay in the apartment alone myself now. I felt a twinge of guilt at the thought of leaving Laura here alone, but I knew I was going to go away on Saturday as planned. Laura would take care of herself. Laura would not be foolish enough to open the door to a stranger.

I frowned as I packed salad in a plastic container. Aunt Emily had been no fool; yet she had apparently opened the door to her murderer. It must mean that Aunt Emily had *known* the man who rang her buzzer at ten after six on Sunday night. Could it have been Tony Bartha? Maybe Tony had come home alone, strangled Aunt Emily in a rage and left in such haste he hadn't stopped to get his belongings or close the door after him. Donald might have come home a little later, discovered the body and fled in panic, afraid that he might be suspected of the murder. But somehow this theory didn't hold up too well. Tony Bartha had struck me as being sly and shiftless, but a cold-blooded killer? That was something else again, wasn't it? And then, all three of the murdered women had belonged to St. Simon's choir. It was too much of a coincidence, wasn't it? My head felt fuzzy and I couldn't think straight. I was going to stop theorizing about the murders. It was in the hands of the police now.

I was putting our cold supper in a bag when I remembered Christmas. I only had two more evenings—not counting tonight—before my trip, and I hadn't distributed all my Christmas gifts or finished the hem on the evening dress I'd made. Tomorrow night I could take care of the gift problem—although it would mean a lot of househopping—and Friday

123

I'd hem my dress and do whatever washing was necessary. Practically everything I was taking was wash-and-wear, so I wouldn't have to worry about ironing on Saturday. I could give Chris his gift tonight since I wouldn't see him again before I left Saturday. I had intended to ask him to drive me to the airport, but considering he'd spent all day Monday and today with me, I couldn't ask him to take more precious time from his writing schedule just to drive me to the airport. I'd had to revise my opinion of Chris a little. I'd thought his writing came first and foremost—that he'd allow nothing to interfere with it. Now I realized that though his writing was very important to him, he wouldn't sacrifice everything and everybody to his career. When the chips were down, Chris could be counted on. How silly that quarrel on Sunday seemed now. How unimportant an afternoon antique-hunting on a day when death came calling. I went to my room, fetched Chris's Christmas gift and told him we were ready to leave.

It was good to be out of the apartment, driving along Queen Mary on a cold, clear night on our way to Chris's place on Côte des Neiges. He had joked that it was the ideal location for a writer—halfway between the hospital and the cemetery. Anyone, he claimed, trying to sustain body and soul by writing needed to be close to one or the other. I'd fallen in love with Chris's living room the first time I'd been in his apartment. A handsome big room with a man-size chesterfield and easy chairs in brown leather and a whole wall full of books. The rich browns of furniture and carpet, the big-scale furniture and the leather upholstery made it a man's room, redolent of tobacco and pipes. There was a smell of snow in the air when we got out of the car on Côte des Neiges. Then we were in Chris's apartment and he was busy putting our dinner on plates while I made coffee. I felt at home here, secure in this environment that bore the stamp of Chris's personality.

It was a complex personality, I thought, if one judged by the paintings he had chosen to grace the walls. Above the chocolate brown chesterfield, a brilliant painting by Amy

124

Dobson made the white wall sing with color. In striking contrast to the boldly executed, life-celebrating Amy Dobson were two prized Picasso prints: "Girl with Mandolin" in a monochrome of browns, and "Child with a Pigeon"; the one so austere, the other so warm and gentle. The boldness, the austerity, the gentleness embodied in the painting and prints were all facets of Christopher Galloway's character. And for further clues to his character, one had only to look at the collection of his own photographs mounted on a huge cork board on one wall. He'd caught the harshness of life, the poetry, the gaiety—in a worn, time-ravaged face; the fairy tracery of snow on bushes and trees; the laughing face of a child plucking a flower. Yes, I would be getting a lot if I married Chris. Aunt Emily had been very fond of him. Always asking me what we were waiting for. Why didn't we get married like sensible people instead of wearing ourselves out trotting back and forth between apartments. But I didn't want to think of Aunt Emily now. Later, a little later, I'd face up to it; but not now.

"You're not eating anything, Nicky. What are you thinking about?"

I picked up my fork and speared a piece of ham. "I was thinking about my trip," I lied. "It seems a bad time to go away and leave Laura, considering what's happened."

Chris looked at me soberly. "Laura will be all right. Don't cancel your plans. You need to get away now. You need to play in the sun and laugh and talk to strangers. Your Aunt Emily wouldn't want you to mourn any more than you can help. She believed that life was for living. So go, Nicky, go on your trip and enjoy yourself. I'll keep in touch with Laura and if she gets too nervous alone in the apartment she can always go and stay with a friend." He rubbed his jaw thoughtfully. "Why don't you suggest that to her? If she stayed with someone while you're gone, you'd both feel better. She can't help but be a little nervous after what's happened."

"I would feel better if she were with someone. Claire St.-

Germaine would probably be glad to have her. I'll ask Laura about it tonight. Do you think they'll get him, Chris?"

"They probably will, with all those men working on the murders, but it may take time. And that detective—the one with the hang-dog expression—"

"Lieutenant Philippe."

"Lieutenant Philippe. He looks too tired to catch anybody."

"I like him, Chris. He may look as though he's going to fall down from exhaustion any second, but I think it's a front. And anyway, he's not working alone. Lieutenant Beaubien may be just a fledgling detective, but to me he looks like a hunter born and bred. The way he sat asking me questions with those black eyes boring into me—he looked like a hawk about to swoop."

"Well, let's hope he swoops soon before anybody else gets murdered." Chris's face was grim; then the strong features relaxed and he spoke in a softer tone. "But let's not think about it any more tonight. Let's talk about us and your trip to Jamaica and the things you're going to see there. I'll get us more coffee first."

We talked for an hour about Jamaica and the things to do and the places to visit there. Chris had visited the Caribbean two years ago. Then I remembered Don Quixote. I picked up the gold and brown parcel lying on the coffee table and handed it to Chris. "Your Christmas gift—this will be the last time I'll see you before I leave."

Chris took the long beribboned package from me, smiling. It was the first time I had seen him smile tonight.

"I was going to take you to the airport on Saturday."

"It's not necessary, Chris. I can easily take a taxi and save you the time."

He looked at me thoughtfully a moment and smiled again. I knew he was thinking about our quarrel on Sunday, but he made no reference to it. I watched him as he carefully removed the ribbon and undid the wrappings of his present. He looked puzzled when he saw the umbrella carton and then his ex-

126

pression changed to one of sheer pleasure as he pulled the melancholy knight from his hiding place.

He patted Don Quixote's metal helmet and beamed at me. "The Knight of the Mournful Countenance—wonderful, Nicky, wonderful. Where did you find him?"

"At the Casa Bella in Place Ville Marie. Actually, I was on my way to my travel agent about my trip to Jamaica and I just happened to spot it in the window. I had to get him. I knew you'd love him."

Chris smiled at the carved wooden figure, got up and looked around. "Where are we going to put him?" Then he walked over to his big mahogany desk with the ancient typewriter on it and plunked the statue down beside the typewriter.

"As a change from rescuing fair damsels and fighting sheep, he can stand guard over my machine and protect its precious output from robbers. Although if he fouls up this job like he does most, I'll probably find him under the desk tomorrow guarding the contents of the wastebasket."

Depressed as I was over my aunt's death, I had to smile at Chris's humor. He came back to the chesterfield and sat down beside me.

"I'm going to miss you when you're gone, Muffet. Three weeks seems a long time to wait to see you again."

"I'll miss you too—and I'll have an answer for you when I get back. Although right now I feel so stunned by Aunt Emily's murder I don't know if I can give the subject the attention it merits. My mind feels so hazy."

He reached over and took my hand. "Your answer can wait another month. Just enjoy yourself in Jamaica. When you come back you can decide. And if your answer is yes, we're going to be married in April."

He was already setting the date. A sudden thrill of fear ran through me. April was just a few months away. The loved face was close to mine, the blue eyes sending depth charges that made everything melt inside me. Why was I afraid?

Chris smiled gently and chanted: "Little Miss Muffet sat on

127

a tuffet, eating her curds and whey, along came a spider and sat down beside her and frightened Miss Muffet away."

I felt annoyed that Chris had read my feelings so accurately. At least now I knew why he looked amused when he called me Muffet.

His face sobered. "It's not only my writing career that bothers you, Nicky. That's just part of it. You're afraid of love. You like the shallows, the quiet waters, but you're afraid of the whirlpools of love. You're afraid of being caught up, whirled away, lost in the maelstrom. But you've got to take chances in life, make an act of faith and surrender yourself to the whirlpool without fear. It's what living's all about, Muffet."

Chris put an arm around me, tilted my chin up with one hand. "I can't instill faith in you. It has to come from you. It has to be your decision. And if you do decide to make the leap of faith, I'll do my best to see you never regret it."

He pulled my head gently down against his shoulder and stroked my hair softly. His voice was an intimate whisper:

" 'Black as a raven's wing is my true love's hair, blue her eyes as Wedgwood . . .' "

Chapter 17

I had intended to give serious thought to what Chris had said to me last night about love, but as it turned out I was too busy to give serious thought to anything. I'd missed three days from work and there was only today and tomorrow left to get everything up to date before I took off for the Caribbean. Miss Eden got Miss Cranston's secretary to give me a hand

128

and I figured that between the two we'd get everything under control by tomorrow.

On my lunch hour I dashed to the Snowdon post office to mail my out-of-town Christmas presents. After my dinner at home I made quick calls with gifts to three different apartments. That took care of everybody except Valerie Randolph. There'd be no time to visit her tomorrow, so I would have to mail her gift. That meant another trip to the post office on my lunch hour tomorrow. I got home from my last call about eleven and was glad to find that Laura was still up. I wanted to talk to her about staying with a friend while I was away. Laura looked thoughtful when I brought the subject up, then shook her head.

"I prefer to stay at home, Nicky. Not that I'm not a little afraid now, but actually I'm more afraid outside than in. I take taxis everywhere at nights now and have the driver come right to the apartment door with me. I'm perfectly safe here as long as I don't open the door to a stranger and for my own peace of mind I'm going to have a peephole installed in the door. I called the owner of the building yesterday and he told me he'd have it looked after right away. So I'll be able to see who's outside and you can bet I won't open the door to a strange face. In fact I won't even reply to the buzzer unless I'm expecting someone. So don't worry, Nicky. If I do get too nervous I can always change my mind and go and stay with Claire or Amy. One thing that does bother me, though, is that man in the lane."

I was a little startled by this last remark of Laura's. I had thought Lieutenant Philippe had taken care of that. "When did you see him?"

"I saw him tonight coming in from school. It's the first time I've seen him since you called that detective about him."

I couldn't recall having seen him either, but then, I hadn't been looking for him and you really had to look sharp to spot him in the dense growth of trees. "I don't like it, Laura. I'm going to call Lieutenant Philippe tomorrow."

129

"I wish you would, Nicky. I don't much like it, either. There's enough to be nervous about now without having strange men lurking in the lane." Laura lit a cigarette and took a nervous puff. "I have to admit, I'll be glad when you get back. It's going to seem strange being alone in the apartment for three weeks. I'll try and write you a couple of times to keep you up to date with what's happening here."

"I'd appreciate it if you would. I'll be anxious to hear of any developments in Aunt Emily's case."

Laura's face was sad. "I know. I'll be sure to let you know, Nicky. I'm going out with Julian Brooks tomorrow night. You won't mind being alone here, will you?"

"No," I lied, "I'll be too busy to notice. I've got a lot to do tomorrow night."

"Is Chris going to drive you to the airport Saturday?"

"No, I told him not to bother. He was with me all day Monday and yesterday and he's trying to get a book finished by the first of February and hasn't any time to waste. I can go by taxi."

"I'll go with you, Nicky. What time does your plane leave?"

"One-forty. But you don't really have to bother, Laura. I don't mind going by myself."

"It's no bother and somebody has to wave goodbye."

"Thanks, Laura, you're a pal." I yawned and got up. "I'm going to bed now. I'm beat from all my rushing around today."

But when I finally got into bed I found I couldn't sleep. Every time I closed my eyes a scene flashed across my mind's eye: a pitiable little figure sprawled on a yellow and white tiled floor, the anguished face turned toward me. I tried to crowd it out with other scenes: golden beaches lapped by azure waters, palm trees, waterfalls, schooners. The pleasant images dissolved before they were fully formed, transformed into Scene One again. Desperately, I opened my eyes wide. As soon as I did, the nightmare picture vanished. I lay for a long time staring into the darkness, thinking of Aunt Emily, and

130

finally the tears came; the tears I'd withheld for four days now. I wept for the cruelty of her death and for my loss. At last the tears were spent. Drained, exhausted, yet somehow at peace, I closed my eyes and fell asleep.

Chapter 18

Friday turned into Saturday so fast it was as though the two days had telescoped. I fairly worked my fingers to the bone at the office on Friday, but by four-thirty all Miss Eden's dictation lay neatly typed on her desk, along with her schedule and appointments for the next month. Everything filable was filed and my desk looked so bare and tidy I could scarcely recognize it as mine. I tried twice to get Lieutenant Philippe to tell him about the man in our lane and on the second try was informed that he was out of town for the weekend. Would I care to leave a number? I left my number and Laura's name. I knew she didn't want to wait three weeks to find out what was going on around our building at nights. When I hung up the phone it occurred to me to wonder how come Lieutenant Philippe could take three-day weekends when there were three unsolved murders on the books.

I had a fast supper Friday night and went to work on my peony-pink dress while Laura got ready for her evening with Julian. As usual, she wasn't ready when her date arrived and I kept him company until Laura, looking slinky and sophisticated in a clingy black dress, put in an appearance. When the two of them left, I went back to my dress, thinking of Julian Brooks. I liked his slightly otherworldly good manners, the faint reserve, the boyishness. I imagined he could be a lot of fun when you got to know him well and Laura was getting to know him well. I hoped something would come of it. Laura was too much of a woman to go through life without a man.

I finished the hem on my dress, pressed it and did my washing. I called Lisa to say goodbye to her and tried to get Valerie Randolph on the phone, but she was out. By that time I was ready to go to bed, but I couldn't. I'd have to stay up until Laura came home because I'd put the chain on the door. Because as far as I was concerned, it wasn't certain that both Aunt Emily and Kathleen Windsor had opened their doors to their murderers. The locks on the doors could have been picked, or jimmied, or whatever it is one does to locks —in such a way that it couldn't be detected after. Of course in Aunt Emily's case someone *had* rung her buzzer at ten after six and she had gone and opened the door to him or her. And that someone was almost certainly her killer. No one had come forward and said they had called on Emily Teasdale the day she was murdered. But there was still a shadow of a doubt. And there was no point in taking any unnecessary chances. I'd leave the chain on the door and stay up till Laura came in. Fortunately for me, she didn't stay out too late. She was in by midnight and I was in bed and asleep fifteen minutes later.

And suddenly it was Saturday, December 11—the long-awaited day—the shine of it tarnished by my aunt's murder. By eleven o'clock I was packed, dressed and ready to go. Chris called to wish me bon voyage and I phoned Valerie to say goodbye. By then it was time for me to leave for the airport. It was a bitterly cold, gray day, typical of December, and my heart should have been singing at leaving it all behind for the sun-kissed Caribbean, but as it was, I could feel only a strange numbness and emptiness. The murder of my aunt weighed heavily on me. Laura waited at the airport with me until my flight was announced and then I was going down the ramp—headed for my plane and three weeks in Jamaica.

Chapter 19

I spent my first week in Jamaica at a small pension in Port Antonio. The first thing I did on arrival was visit the local tourist board to enroll in the meet-the-people program. They introduced me to two Jamaican girls my own age and they in turn introduced me to their friends. So I never lacked for company that first week away from home and that was the way I wanted it. I didn't want time alone to think—to think of what had happened in Montreal a short week ago. My new Jamaican friends took me into their homes and hearts, introduced me to their customs, their history, their pleasures.

Together we visited the Blue Hole—six miles east of Port Antonio—went rafting down the Rio Grande on a bamboo raft, rode the beautiful trails up into the Blue Mountains, visited a Maroon village, spent sunny hours swimming and water skiing. I went to market with a Jamaican friend's cook, was introduced to all kinds of Jamaican vegetables and fruits —chochos, yampies, soursops, Otaheite apples. I sipped coconut water, ate breadfruit obligingly hauled down from a tree for me, listened to stories of duppies of dead relatives come back to haunt.

The week flew by, so taken up with people and activities I didn't have time to think of anything. And then it was on to Kingston and the Terra Nova hotel, small but with a reputation for good service and good food. Again I applied to the local tourist board for the names of girls who would show me around their city. And again I found myself welcomed wholeheartedly, treated as a long-lost friend. I was taken to

see Devon House, Port Royal's Fort Charles, Spanish Town
—the oldest city on the island—the Arawak Indian Museum
a few miles from Spanish Town. I was escorted to a number
of art galleries—amazed to find so many artists of high caliber
concentrated in one place. I saw a performance of the Jamaica
National Dance Company, listened to calypso music, ate at
Kingston's favorite Jamaica-style restaurant, the Humming-
bird. And one warm, starlit night I put on my peony-pink
evening dress and made the acquaintance of Kingston's night
life—noisy, gay, sophisticated. I danced with a dark, handsome stranger who wanted to see me again, but I wasn't in the
mood for flirtations—and besides—he didn't measure up to
Chris. I didn't think I'd ever find a man to measure up to
Chris. On my sixth day in Kingston I received a letter from
Laura. I read it in the terrace dining room while I ate lunch:

Friday, Dec. 17th

Dear Nicky:

We've been having sleet, snow, rain and cold ever since you
left. Now doesn't that make you feel good from where you sit?
Enjoy yourself while you can because there's lots more sleet,
snow, etc., coming. Lieut. Philippe called me on Monday. He
told me that that man in the lane is police—from the Narcotics
Squad. Someone in the building is trafficking in heroin. Small
fish, according to your detective but they're hoping some bigger
fish will be lured into the net. Nice neighborhood we live in,
eh? But I'm relieved to know it's police. We don't have to worry
any more about *that!* Lieut. Philippe said he was sorry he didn't
tell you but he was so busy it slipped his mind. I asked him if
there were any leads in your Aunt Emily's case and he said
nothing very hopeful—they are working in the dark. They have
strong suspicions about George Matrai and are still searching for
him. Lieut. Philippe says the Narcotics Squad are keeping their
eyes open for Tony Bartha, too. He's suspected of heroin dealing, but they haven't been able to catch him with the goods.

I had a nice letter from your Aunt May, thanking me for the
use of the apartment when she was here. Your pine armoire and
the motorcycle were delivered here last Saturday just after I got

134

home from the airport. The armoire is a beautiful piece of furniture. Chris has called a couple of times to see how things are. He really misses you, Nicky. If you don't marry him you should have your head read.

I've been out with Julian Brooks several times since you left and am liking him more each time. I really enjoy his company. He's always ready to try anything new. We've been eating in funny little restaurants in some of the most unlikely places but they've all been very good. And would you believe, this weekend we're going to Jay Peak to *ski*—of all things! Julian's never tried it either and he says it should be interesting! Broken legs don't seem that interesting to me but I'm game if he is. And I'm looking forward to the Après Ski! Sybil Hepworth finds Julian *very* interesting. I've caught her peeking out the crack of her door every time he's called for me.

And guess who I saw coming out of St. Simon's Church on Girouard last Monday? Or rather the parish house next door to the church. T. Oliphant, if I'm not mistaken! My taxi had stopped for a red light and was just starting up again when someone coming out of the house caught my eye. If it wasn't Oliphant, it certainly looked like him. Although he wasn't carrying his identifying mark—the brown carton.

This is it for now, Nicky. Will write again if there is anything interesting to report. When you send a postcard be sure to let me know what flight you're returning on.

Love
Laura

I folded the letter up thoughtfully and put it in the new straw bag I'd bought in Port Antonio. So Laura had seen T. Oliphant coming out of the pastor's house. Did that mean he was a member of St. Simon's Church? And if he was a member, why did it disturb me so much? Lieutenant Philippe had advanced the theory that if the slayer of all three victims was one and the same, he was likely a member of St. Simon's. But the mere fact that our neighbor belonged to the church didn't mean a thing in itself. Why then did a chill descend on me on this sunny terrace in the Caribbean when Laura introduced T.

135

Oliphant into her letter? Something nagged at the back of my mind. I concentrated hard all through the rest of my lunch, but I couldn't coax it into consciousness. But somehow, my day had been spoiled by the contents of Laura's letter. I glanced at my watch and got up from the table. I was meeting Mildred and Annie—two Jamaican teachers—for a shopping expedition to Spanish Court. I was trying to find something to take home to Laura and Chris and I also intended to have a couple of pair of sandals made up for myself. I already had a gift for Lisa—a set of large pewter serving spoons, wrapped in suede, which I'd found at Things Jamaican. Mildred had pointed them out as an excellent buy. I hoped I could do as well by Laura and Chris.

I'd saved the most touristy part of the island—Montego Bay—for the last week of my vacation. And I'd splurged on accommodations there. My home in Montego Bay was a plush hotel set beside a curve of dazzling white sand, fringed with hibiscus, frangipani and coconut palms. My big bedroom had a spacious balcony facing on the sea, where I took a leisurely breakfast each day and planned the day's activities. Usually I spent the mornings on the beach and the afternoons sight-seeing. Then came late dinners on the beach terrace and dancing to the throb of steel bands.

The week in Montego Bay was the laziest of the three, but I still managed to see a number of interesting things. I saw Rose Hall, of course, the home of the notorious Anna Palmer, known as the White Witch of Rose Hall; and Good Hope, one of the island's greatest surviving houses, twenty miles east of Montego Bay. I visited several other estates and a sugar plantation; studied Arawak cave paintings at Kempshot, ten miles southeast of Montego Bay; I visited the bird sanctuary at Rockland and saw everything from saffron finches to banana quits; I strolled through the beautiful Georgian colonial town of Falmouth and hired a boat at Oyster Bay on a dark night and discovered that anything that moved on the water —hands, oars, ripples—left a phosphorescent trail of pale fire

136

that slowly disappeared. And I found the perfect gift for Laura—a fabulous dashiki shirt. I was so taken with the colorful batik prints I bought one for myself as well.

The three weeks in Jamaica rushed by and although I had intended to give serious thought to the question of Chris and myself, I suddenly found to my amazement it was time to go home and I hadn't done any thinking at all on the all-important subject of whether or not I should marry Chris. But he had said my decision could wait for a month, so I wasn't going to worry about it. I felt refreshed, relaxed after my three weeks in the sun, and I had a feeling that when I got back to Montreal I'd be able to put things in their proper perspective and come to a decision without further vacillation.

I had a short note from Laura the day before I left Jamaica. It was dated December 27 and reported that on December 20 there had been another strangling murder in Montreal. The murder occurred in an apartment on Queen Mary Road, near Godfrey—which is just a block east of Winnicott. The woman had been forty-six years of age and had lived alone. The body was discovered when a neighbor investigated after seeing the victim's morning delivery of milk still outside her door at seven at night. There had been a public outcry in Montreal when the news of the fourth murder in the district in a month hit the newspapers. The police had appealed to women living alone not to talk to strangers or open their doors to strangers. And the police asked the public to come forward with any information that might be helpful in tracking down the killer. Police officials were now of the opinion that all four murders were the work of one man—a psychopath.

I shuddered involuntarily as I read Laura's letter, written in her small, neat handwriting. Another murder—just two weeks after Aunt Emily's—and it had taken place in a building just a ten-minute walk away from home. They were all older women. Kathleen Windsor, the youngest of the lot, had been thirty-eight. Was it some deranged person who saw hated

137

"mother" images in the women he murdered? Although it would be hard to cast childish Kathleen Windsor in the mother role. Still, it was odd that they were all older women. But I hadn't read enough of Freud or his disciples to theorize along psychological lines. I only hoped there soon would be some break in the murder cases. Because, judging by the statement issued by the police, it looked as though they feared the murders would continue until the killer was caught. At the end of her letter Laura confessed that she had been frightened enough by news of the latest slaying to move in with Claire St.-Germaine. She had been at Claire's since December 21, when word of the murder appeared in the paper.

There was another disquieting note in her letter. Laura had been getting what she called "breathy" phone calls ever since I had left Montreal. The phone would ring three or four times, but when she answered all she heard over the receiver was heavy breathing. Normally, Laura said in her letter, this wouldn't have bothered her much—there were all kinds of weirdos in a big city—but on top of the shock of Aunt Emily's murder, it had unnerved her. She hoped, by the time I arrived home, the calls would have stopped. While she was at Claire's, she of course couldn't answer her phone and she figured the silent caller would get discouraged and give up after a week or so. Reading between the lines of Laura's letter, I got the decided impression she'd be relieved to have me home again. She added a postscript at the bottom of her letter. Chris had to go to Toronto the weekend of December 31 and she and Julian Brooks would meet my plane tomorrow. I was in a sober mood when I put the letter away. When would the killings stop?

Chapter 20

Fast-falling snow obscured my view from the plane window as we touched down at Montreal International Airport. I fished a pair of plastic overshoes from my tote bag and slipped them on ruefully. There'd be no more walking about in sandals for a while. There weren't many people on the plane and it took just fifteen minutes to claim my bag and get through Customs. Laura and Julian were waiting in the small crowd near the entrance to the airport. They gave me broad welcome-home smiles.

"You've got a marvelous tan, Nicky. You'll look more than ever like the Egyptian to Chris."

Julian took my bag from me. "You look smashing, Nicky. I hope you had a good time?"

"I did, Julian, but it's good to be back—be it ever so frigid, there's no place like home." I looked at the winter-pale faces around me. "Everybody here looks a little sick."

Laura laughed. "Don't rub it in. Not everybody can take three-week holidays in the Caribbean in the winter."

Julian smiled his engaging boyish smile. "If you're not too tired, we'd like you to come to my place for a drink to celebrate your home coming. We won't keep you out late, just an hour or two."

"I'm not too tired, Julian, and I think it's a nice way to celebrate my return."

He looked pleased. "Good. My car's in the parking lot. Shall we get started?"

Half an hour later we got out of Julian's sleek black

Porsche in front of a triangular steel and glass structure in Westmount. We hurried across the broad snow-swept plaza into the warmth and luxury of Somerset Place.

Julian Brooks's apartment on the second floor of the building was done in sophisticated pale tones of beige, taupe and putty—à la Syrie Maugham. The big combination living room-library featured sleek modular furniture and a lot of chrome and glass. Through a partly open plexiglass room divider I caught a glimpse of a dining area with rosewood table and buffet. There were several small metal and marble sculptures in the living room and a Henrick Weiler landscape brooded over the beige love seat. Julian must do well as a furniture designer, I thought, to afford a setup like this.

Laura and I talked in the living room while Julian fixed drinks in the kitchen.

"It's good to have you home, Nicky, and it's going to be good to sleep in my own bed tonight. Claire's a wonderful hostess, but there's still nothing like your own apartment."

"I know how you feel, Laura. I'm looking forward to going home tonight, too. I don't suppose you heard anything from that Lieutenant Beaubien who was assisting on Aunt Emily's case—or Lieutenant Philippe?"

"Not a word from either one. And there's been nothing in the newspapers. It looks as though the police are up against a blank wall. But we did hear from somebody else, or rather Chris did. Donald Hammill."

"Donald's come back! When? And how did he get on to Chris?"

"He came back a week ago, but Chris didn't tell me until after I'd written you. Remember he was at our place the night of his birthday when Chris was there? He just went through the phone book and called all the Galloways listed until he hit on the right one. Apparently Chris and Donald had a good talk the night they were both at our apartment and the boy really took to Chris. The poor kid was frightened stiff. Thought the police were after him. He counted on Chris to make everything all right again. And so far he hasn't been disappointed. First thing Chris did was to persuade Donald to talk to the police so he wouldn't have to go around expecting a hand on his shoulder any second. And the second thing Chris did was to persuade the police to question Donald at his apartment, rather than taking him in for questioning. Donald felt a lot more secure talking to the police in Chris's apartment, with Chris standing by him. Donald was interviewed by both Lieutenant Beaubien of Homicide and a detective from the Narcotics Squad. He succeeded in convincing the police that he knew nothing of Aunt Emily's murder and that he didn't know where Tony Bartha was. The police told Chris they were satisfied with the statement Donald had given them and that he wouldn't be bothered again."

"I'm glad Donald came back. And that Chris stood by him. Did Donald go back to the apartment that Sunday with Tony and discover Aunt Emily's body?"

"No. Tony and Donald left your aunt's apartment together that day, but once outside they split up. Donald came back to the apartment about six-thirty. When he couldn't get an answer to his ring he buzzed another apartment to gain entry to the inner lobby. He found your aunt's door open and walked right in. He was shocked and horrified when he discovered the body. He thought Tony had done it because your aunt had asked him to leave. Donald was too frightened to think clearly. He was afraid he would be implicated in the murder and he took to his heels. He was sleeping in an abandoned house in the East End with a couple of hippies, but the feeling of being hunted was wearing him down and finally he plucked up his courage and called Chris."

"Where is Donald staying now?"

"With Chris. He's agreed to be responsible for Donald until he can be placed in a boy's home. Donald's name is near the top of the list and he shouldn't have to wait long."

I smiled to myself. The man in my life could put on a gruff, cynical front, but he had the heart of a marshmallow. Here he

141

was playing big brother to a troubled adolescent when he had so little time to spare. The deadline for his book was only a month away. I wondered how he could get any writing at all done with Donald there carrying on a love affair with a guitar. Again I had to concede that Chris was not as single-minded about his writing as I'd thought. The door buzzer broke into my thoughts and Julian came out to answer it. I was surprised when he came back a minute later wheeling a small trolley cart. He removed the white cloth covering the top with a flourish.

"Food," he said enthusiastically, lifting plates from the cart and putting them on the big glass coffee table. "I thought we should make a little party of the occasion."

I looked with interest at the array of food now ornamenting the coffee table. There were olives, pickles, sausage rolls, fancy sandwiches and miniature French pastries.

"It looks good, Julian, but where did it all come from?"

"From the hotel restaurant. They run a catering service for the tenants. It's one of the many things I like about this place. You can cook your own meals, eat in the restaurant or have food sent in. And there's maid service, of course, so you get all the comforts of home but still have complete privacy. Tuck into the food, girls, I'll bring the drinks in."

Julian left the room, walking with the light, easy stride of an athlete. He wasn't handsome, I decided; his face was too long and thin. But he was certainly attractive, exuding an air of well-bred masculinity. He was back a minute later with our drinks and the three of us settled down to enjoy ourselves. Laura and Julian had a hundred questions to ask about my trip and when we'd exhausted that subject, Julian brought up his trip to Rome next week.

"Are you going on business?" I asked.

"Yes, Nicky. I'm going to see an Italian furniture designer, Giorgio Bartoli. We're going to wrap up our plans for going into business together. I'm buying up a furniture plant that closed down in Lashute, and Giorgio and I are going to design, market and manufacture our own furniture."

142

"What kind of furniture, Julian?"

"Home furniture made of plastic. I've been studying the market for a year now and plastic is the coming thing. That's how I met Giorgio; Italy pioneered in the use of plastic, and Giorgio Bartoli is one of the foremost Italian furniture designers. I met him at a designers' forum in Rome last year. We're anxious to get things rolling." Julian's eyes were bright with enthusiasm.

"But isn't plastic sort of a trendy thing? Maybe it will be out by next year."

"Not at all, Nicky. It's the fastest-growing structural material being designed today. A few years ago there was only a little plastic used in furniture, but in 1970 approximately eight hundred million pounds of plastic were used in furniture production in the U.S. and consumers at the Montreal Furniture Market last August were very enthusiastic about the plastic furniture displayed. It's got everything going for it. It's multi-functional, easy to care for, lightweight and lighthearted. It fits in with the life-styles of today's young moderns. And when you consider that forty-five per cent of the population is under thirty, you've got a big market for it." Julian paused and smiled. "I'm afraid I get carried away if I'm not stopped."

Laura smiled at me. "Next to sailing, it's his favorite subject." She turned to Julian. "We don't mind listening, dear. If you've got more to say, say it and get it out of your system."

Julian's smile was broader. "Well, if I may add something, I'd like to say that plastic is beautiful to work with—one can create such clean, free-flowing lines with it—and our designs are going to highlight plastic in its pure form. We want to show plastic as plastic, not as an imitation of wood or any other material. And we're going to use the vacuum forming process in manufacturing. It utilizes—Julian stopped, sat up straighter and set his glass down. "I say, I've gone too far. Change the subject, Laura."

Laura and I laughed at the penitent look on his face.

143

"Go and get us another drink, dear, and all will be forgiven."

Julian got up quickly. "I'm sorry, girls, I hadn't even noticed that your glasses were empty."

He was back with our drinks a minute later, still looking contrite. Laura grinned at him teasingly and he smiled back, sending a secret message with his gray-green eyes. Green eyes and gray-green eyes had been sending signals all evening. And I hadn't missed Laura's use of "dear" when she addressed Julian. Something was doing between them, I thought with approval.

He speared an olive with a toothpick and looked at Laura. "I just had an idea. Why don't we ask Nicky and Chris to join us next Saturday at the Club Midnight? It would be fun to make a foursome. And then you wouldn't have to go home alone."

"That's a great idea. What about it, Nicky? We're going to see a Spanish dance company at the Club Midnight. Julian's plane to Rome leaves Saturday night at twelve-forty, so I was going to go home alone in a taxi. I know you're not as crazy about flamenco as I am, but I'm sure you'll like this performance. It's a classical ballet company and it's been getting rave reviews."

"I think I'd enjoy it, Laura. But I'll have to ask Chris if he can make it for Saturday."

Julian lit a cigarette for Laura. "You ask him, Nicky, and let me know so I can change our reservations. I'll have to do it soon. I think it's going to be a sellout."

"I'll let you know as soon as I can. Did Chris say when he'd be back in Montreal, Laura?"

"He said he'd be back about ten tomorrow night. He'll call you when he gets in."

Julian glanced at his watch. "Here I promised to keep Nicky out only an hour or so and it's after twelve now. I think it's time I took you home." He got up decisively and

Laura and I followed suit. I'd enjoyed our evening but was glad to be going home now after three weeks away.

Twenty minutes later Julian deposited my bag on the living room floor of our apartment, gave Laura and me a military salute and was gone.

We changed into night clothes, curled up on the sofa and talked another hour before going to bed. Among other things, we talked about Julian. Laura had been out with him half a dozen times in the three weeks I'd been away and admitted to liking him more each time.

"If I keep seeing him," she commented lightly, "I might end up falling in love with him."

My private opinion was that Laura was already in love with Julian Brooks but was trying to deny her real feelings. She had been hurt deeply by the breakup with Carl and was still a little afraid to trust her own feelings. But I was counting on Julian to make Laura forget her former love.

"How did you like Julian's apartment?" Laura asked.

"Veddy, veddy elegant. The rent must be astronomical. And he's buying a furniture plant. Furniture designing must be a lucrative business."

"The top designers do well and I think Julian fits in that category, although he'd be too modest to admit it. And then he owned an apartment building which he's selling for one hundred thousand. That's where the money is coming from for the furniture plant. Julian will make a success of it, too. He's a clever cookie." Laura yawned and stretched. "It is good to have you back, Nicky. I was so frightened by that last murder I couldn't take being alone here."

I nodded soberly. "It gave me a shock when I read your letter. Four murders in a month is a pretty grim score. You know, I sort of wondered if Tony Bartha had killed Aunt Emily, but when I heard about the latest strangling murder I came to the conclusion it couldn't have been Tony—that it's one man who's done them all. I wonder if the latest victim— what was the name, Laura?"

145

"Cassidy. Eileen Cassidy."

"I wonder if she happened to be a member of St. Simon's choir?"

"I wondered that myself. There wasn't much in the paper. Just a few lines the day after the murder and then nothing more. I have an idea that the police are trying to play it down to prevent panic. I've talked to a few people in this building who are pretty nervous. One woman upstairs said she was going to get a police dog. I told her the landlord wouldn't permit dogs, but she said that wasn't going to make any difference to her—she had a right to protect her life." Laura bit her lip and punched the pillow beside her. "Every time I think of your Aunt Emily—"

"I know, Laura. I managed to avoid thinking about it for three whole weeks in Jamaica. But now that I'm home where there are memories . . . Let's just pray they get the devil."

Chapter 21

Chris called when he got home from Toronto Sunday night and we made a date to stage the big reunion scene on Monday at the Carmen Espresso, a coffeehouse with Spanish decor. It was cheap—something to bear in mind when your escort is a struggling young writer—cheerful and lively, and we both liked the Irish Coffee Maison—an interesting brew of scotch, Drambuie, Tia Maria and whipped cream. Chris was agreeable to going on a foursome with Laura and Julian next Saturday and I passed the good word to Laura to tell Julian.

When Chris picked me up Monday night after work I was

146

wearing a sleeveless white wool which set off to perfection the mahogany tan I'd brought back from Jamaica. He gave me an ebullient hug, then stood back and made a low obeisance. "You look like an Egyptian goddess made flesh," he said with approval. Then he helped me on with my coat, giving me another jubilant hug in the process. I felt the warm blood rush to my face and my heart quickened with the surge of love that charged through me. It was an excited, happy, frightening love this love I had for Christopher Galloway.

There was a fair crowd at the Carmen Espresso on Stanley when we got there at seven, but we managed to find a corner table. Between bites of Wiener Schnitzel, I gave Chris the highlights of my trip to Jamaica. Then we turned to affairs in Montreal.

"How long do you think you'll have Donald Hammill with you, Chris?"

"The authorities said they'd have a place for him in a home within a week or two."

"It was good of you to stand by him."

His voice was gruff. "What else could I do, he had nowhere to turn? And your Aunt Emily would have liked me to keep an eye out for the kid. But I'll be glad when I can unload him on somebody else. I worried the whole damn weekend I was in Toronto about leaving him alone. He's a good kid but so naïve and impressionable he could get into trouble a block from home. Apparently Tony Bartha persuaded Donald to try heroin once and he didn't like it. Tony held that like a sword over Donald's head. Threatened to tell the police Donald had taken heroin if he ever breathed a word of getting heroin from Tony. Poor Donald actually believed he could be arrested on somebody's say-so without any evidence. Donald had a good idea Tony was a drug pusher, but he didn't know where he was getting the stuff from. He looked the other way so he wouldn't see anything. He was that scared of Tony Bartha."

147

"Do you think Donald knows where Tony is but was afraid to tell the police?"

"No, I think Donald leveled with me. He hasn't a clue where Bartha is."

"What does Donald do all day while you're writing?"

Chris grinned. "He works as a disk jockey in a music store. I just happened to know the owner. And since it's music, Donald doesn't consider it work. He's thrilled to be earning some money. The nights I'm teaching or out with you he can play his guitar to his heart's content. We worked things out pretty well between us. But I'll still be relieved to hand him over to somebody else. I wasn't cut out to be a nursemaid." Chris scowled as he made this last remark to show me how tough he was and I smiled to myself. Chris cared what happened to Donald Hammill.

It was over our Irish Coffee Maison that I remembered Aunt Emily's motorcycle and I told Chris to tell Donald it was his if he wanted it. Chris said Donald would probably be thrilled to have it and no doubt would be on my doorstep tomorrow night to claim it.

"How's the book coming, Chris?"

He grimaced. "I'm getting there, but I'm going to have to burn some midnight oil to make the deadline. Not to mention early dawn oil. I'm starting work at seven these mornings." He glanced at his watch. "All right if we go now, Muffet?"

He was looking at me, but he didn't really see me. He was thinking about his book. He had greeted me so eagerly tonight, happy to see me home; now he was miles away. I felt the old, familiar sensation of rejection. Would I ever get used to it? Was I willing to get used to it? I smiled and said lightly, "I'm ready when you are, Chris."

Chapter 22

Valerie Randolph phoned me Tuesday night. Her voice, which had been as bubbly as a brook when she was singing the praises of Paul Hanna a month ago, had gone flat. Tearfully she informed me that Paul Hanna had turned out to be a Grade-A louse. He had led her down the primrose path and when she couldn't find the vine-covered cottage at the end of it, she'd taken off her rose-colored glasses to see better. And of course she had. But as I said, Valerie is one of those unfortunates who has to learn the hard way. I hate people who say "I told you so," so I refrained from saying it. Instead I commiserated with her on the prevalence of two-legged predators and suggested she swallow her pride and give Peter a call. After all, it was a silly quarrel that had come between them and chances were Peter would jump at the opportunity to make up. Valerie listened with respect to what I had to say and I could hear the hope grow in her voice. She said goodbye with such eagerness I got the idea she could hardly wait to get off the phone so she could call Peter. Silently I wished her luck.

That was Tuesday night and there wasn't anything else worthy of note until Thursday night. I had my dinner downtown after work and went to Marshall's Fabric House looking for bargains. Most of their winter fabrics went on sale in January and I made it a point to shop for next winter's dress materials in January. I found some terrific values in woolens and left Marshall's at eight-thirty, loaded down with bags and very well pleased with my shopping expedition. I walked

149

toward Dorchester to get the 62 bus, turning my coat collar up against the sub-zero cold. I had gone just a block when I met Guy Sabourin. He turned on the ever-ready smile and greeted me effusively.

"Nicky! Welcome home! You look wonderful!"

"Thanks, Guy. I was going to call Lisa tonight to find out how the two of you survived my absence."

Guy laughed. "We managed, Nicky, but only just. Say, how about having a cup of coffee with me? I want to show you something."

I was anxious to get home, but Guy's dark handsome face was lit with such eagerness I didn't have the heart to say no. So I said yes and in a few minutes we were seated across from each other in Pepy's Coffee House, drinking coffee.

Guy asked a few perfunctory questions about my trip, then fumbled in his coat pocket. He produced a small Birks jewelry bag, from which he took a little velvet case. He handed the case to me, his dark eyes flashing with excitement.

"It's for Lisa's birthday, Nicky. Do you think she'll like it?"

It was an antique gold pendant set with a generous-sized sapphire, encircled by pearls. Knowing the value of sapphires, I looked at the pendant with a certain amount of awe. Lisa had wondered where the money had come from for the magnificent mink Guy had bought just a short time ago and the new Mercedes-Benz. And now another extravagant gift.

"It's a beautiful piece of jewelry, Guy. Lisa should love it."

"You *really* think she'll like it?" His smile was anxious. "I didn't know whether to get her a pendant or a ring."

"She'll like it," I assured him—wishing I could tell him that his grandiose gestures gave Lisa more concern than pleasure. His anxious smile relaxed into the pleased grin of a little boy who has an apple for the teacher.

"Nothing's too good for her, Nicky. She's a wonderful girl. I'm always afraid I'll go home one day and find her gone."

150

There was Guy's insecurity speaking. It was pretty obvious that he found it hard to believe that Lisa loved him. Hence the too-lavish gifts. Guy was trying to buy Lisa's love. But where was he getting the money? I had the feeling that Lisa had reason to be concerned about that question.

Guy put his coffee cup down and stroked his spade beard thoughtfully. "How's Chris?" he asked.

"He's a little frazzled right now. He's only got a month to finish his book and it makes him pretty edgy."

Guy smiled pleasantly, but the smile didn't reach his eyes. "Chris takes too much out of himself with his books. After all, he's only writing for entertainment."

Translated that read: Chris is writing froufrou, which doesn't take any talent, while I'm doing serious work—writing plays of social significance. He's not in the same class as I am.

I swallowed the barb, smiled sweetly and changed the subject. When we left the restaurant a few minutes later I was thoroughly irritated with Guy Sabourin. I could have quarreled with him in the restaurant but avoided it for Lisa's sake. And all the way home on the bus I pondered the question of where Guy got the money for minks, Mercedes-Benzes and sapphires.

Chapter 23

It was a bitterly cold day again Friday and I shivered my way to work and home again, thankful that the weekend had at last arrived. Getting back into harness after relaxing for three weeks under a Caribbean sun had been rather painful. I was in a happy frame of mind when I shut our apartment door behind me—or in as happy a frame of mind as was possible, considering my favorite aunt had been murdered just a month ago. I'd kept myself frantically busy in Jamaica to avoid thinking about it, but now that I was home, in surroundings once frequented by Aunt Emily, she came to mind unbidden in the small, quiet moments of time when I was alone and unoccupied in the apartment. And tonight I would be alone in the apartment. Laura was staying downtown for dinner and shopping. I felt the happy frame of mind slipping away. Resolutely I made a mental list of things to do. I'd make myself a full-course meal, instead of the soup and sandwich I usually had when Laura was out for dinner; I'd finish unpacking my bag and wash the clothes I'd taken to Jamaica with me; I'd give myself my weekly beauty treatment tonight instead of tomorrow; and if there was any time left over before Laura got home, I'd begin reading the Book-of-the-Month selection which had arrived yesterday. And while I was busy with chores I'd think about our date tomorrow at the Club Midnight. It was going to be a lot of fun.

By ten o'clock I'd accomplished everything I'd set myself and Laura still wasn't home. I got a roaring fire going in the living room and settled down on the sofa with *The Nixon Recession Caper*. I'd only been reading five minutes when the phone rang. Maybe it was Chris. But all I heard when I picked up the phone was heavy breathing.

"Hello!" I said sharply. In reply I got more heavy breathing. "Hello!" I said again, feeling suddenly frightened. The labored breathing sounded sinister. Still no reply but deep, drawn-out breathing.

I hung up and stood staring at the phone as if it had grown horns. It's nothing to get upset about, I told myself firmly. Nobody could do me any harm over the telephone. But he was a persistent devil. He hadn't been discouraged by Laura's ten-day absence from the apartment. I was going to suggest to her that she have the phone number changed to an unlisted number. That would put a stop to the nuisance.

152

I went back to the living room and my book, feeling a little on edge. I wished Laura would come home. Where had she gotten to? The stores closed at nine. I couldn't have been reading more than fifteen minutes when there was a soft knocking on the door. I jumped up, startled. Who could it be at almost ten-thirty at night? Had Laura forgotten her keys? My soft-soled slippers made no sound on the thick carpet as I walked to the front hall. I was glad that Laura had had a peephole put in the door.

My heart skipped a beat when I looked through it. Outside was T. Oliphant, his strange eyes looking even more sinister through the magnifying lens in the peephole. My heart jumping wildly, I stepped back from the door and flattened myself against the wall, forgetting that he couldn't see me through the glass. The soft knocking was repeated. I cringed against the wall, trying to fight down the panic. T. Oliphant terrified me and there he was outside my door and me alone in the apartment. I wasn't going to answer his knock. I wondered if he could see light through the crack in the door—if he knew I was inside the apartment, cowering with fear. With an effort I gained mastery over the terror that had taken possession of me. There was a locked door between us. He couldn't harm me unless I opened that door and if I waited long enough he would go away. I must have stood for five minutes, not moving from my post against the wall. Then I gained courage and looked through the peephole again. He was gone. With an immense sigh of relief I went back to the living room and threw more wood on the fire. Then I sat cross-legged on the floor in front of the fireplace, feeling somehow protected by the bright leaping flames. What did T. Oliphant want with me and why had I reacted with stark terror when I'd seen him at the door? Suddenly I remembered Laura's last letter to me while I was in Jamaica. She had reported seeing our strange neighbor coming out of the parish house next to St. Simon's Church. And Lieutenant Philippe had suggested that the killer of Elsie Grunberger,

153

Kathleen Windsor and Aunt Emily might be a member of St. Simon's Church. Even though it appeared that Oliphant was a member of the church, that did not make him a murderer. But something had bugged me when I'd read Laura's letter . . . something about Oliphant that I hadn't been able to dredge up from memory. Now I had it, and with it came a fresh surge of fear. Kathleen Windsor had been at our apartment the night she was murdered. We'd passed Oliphant in the hall when we were leaving the building and our stooped, gray-faced neighbor had fixed his frightening glittery glare on Kathleen's pants. And two nights before Aunt Emily was murdered she'd been in our apartment, and again we'd met Oliphant at the door when she was leaving. Her knickers had been the object of the same wild, intense look he'd given Kathleen Windsor's pants. Both times his thin mouth had pursed with disgust. And I'd gotten the same treatment from him the Saturday I met him at the mailbox when I was wearing my corduroys. It was obvious he couldn't stand seeing women in pants, and Laura and I had long ago come to the conclusion that he was a woman-hater. Was his hatred so great he would kill? He *did* act strange and he was apparently a member of St. Simon's Church. But neither Aunt Emily nor Kathleen Windsor have given any sign of recognizing him when they'd passed him on their way out. But that didn't mean that Oliphant didn't know them. Maybe he did work around the church. In that capacity he wouldn't have been introduced to them but would have become familiar with them seeing them. It still didn't explain how he gained access to Kathleen Windsor's and Aunt Emily's apartments. But they might have opened their doors to him because they remembered seeing him at the church, even though they didn't know his name.

T. Oliphant had made a point of avoiding both Laura and me when we met him in the lobby. And now he was knocking on my door at half-past ten at night. I didn't like it, I didn't like it at all. I was going to call Lieutenant Philippe. It wasn't likely he'd be in his office at this hour, so it would have to wait until morning. But I was going to call him first thing. I was deathly afraid of our mysterious neighbor.

Restlessly I roamed the living room, too edgy now to read. When I heard the key in the lock my heart jumped again. That would be Laura of course, but I found myself hurrying to the door and peering through the peephole again. Laura's glossy red head, bent over the keyhole, was a welcome sight. She looked surprised when she opened the door and found me standing there.

"What is it, Nicky? You look so . . . so relieved."

"Oh, I am, Laura, you'll never know *how* relieved! But I'll wait till you get rid of your coat and parcels before I tell you about it."

A few minutes later we were sitting together in the living room and I was telling Laura about our neighbor's surprise visit and how frightened I was. She looked puzzled.

"The man avoids us like the plague. I can't imagine why he'd come to our apartment tonight. I think you were wise not to open the door, Nicky. There's something about that man that frightens me."

I nodded in agreement and proceeded to tell Laura about the times when Oliphant had glared at Kathleen Windsor and Aunt Emily.

She frowned and spoke thoughtfully. "It mightn't mean anything and again it might mean a whole lot. One thing is certain. T. Oliphant hates women."

"I'm going to call Lieutenant Philippe in the morning. He may think I'm losing my grip, but I don't care what he thinks as long as he investigates that man."

Then I remembered the breathy phone call. Laura looked annoyed when I told her about it.

"I thought he'd have given up by now. I'll call the Bell on Monday and ask for an unlisted number. Between one thing and another you haven't had a very pleasant evening."

"What about you, Laura. How did your shopping go?"

155

"I found just what I was looking for at Desjardin's. And then I met one of the girls from the office in the store and we went to a restaurant to warm up on coffee. Both of us were half-frozen."

Laura picked up a gold and black dress box and started to open it. "I thought an evening of Spanish dancing with Julian and you and Chris deserved something special and I really splurged on this."

She unfolded from a nest of tissue a jade-green velvet dress with a low scoop neckline and long narrow sleeves. Her face flushed now with excitement, Laura held the dress up in front of her. The color was stunning with her fair complexion and gleaming red hair. I stroked the luxurious velvet pile admiringly.

"It's beautiful! Julian will love you in it."

She spoke laughingly, but her flush had deepened. I hope so, Nicky. He'll be away in Rome for four whole days and I want to give him something to remember me by."

I grinned teasingly. "He'll never forget the redhead in the jade green dress."

Laura smiled back and her green eyes glowed. "I'm going to call it a day. I'll have to get up early tomorrow. I've got a lot to do."

"I'm getting up early too. I want to get Lieutenant Philippe before he leaves his office. I won't rest easy until he does some checking on T. Oliphant."

Chapter 24

When I got up at eight-thirty on Saturday morning Laura was already finishing her breakfast in the kitchen. I had a cup of coffee with her to wake myself up and then I went to call Lieutenant Philippe. He had told me he usually went to his office for an hour or so on Saturdays and I hoped this was one of the Saturdays he was there. I didn't think I could wait until Monday for someone to do something about our neighbor. I was in luck. The detective was in. Speaking slowly and matter-of-factly, so he wouldn't think I was a hysterical female, I told him of T. Oliphant's strange behavior with Kathleen Windsor, Aunt Emily and myself, of his visit to the apartment last night and of my fears and suspicions concerning him. The detective listened without interruption until I'd finished my story; then he spoke politely, in his soft Gallic voice.

"Mademoiselle, your neighbor may not like women wearing pants, but that does not mean he is going to murder them. He may not like women. He may even hate them, as his behavior seems to suggest, but this does not make him a murderer. And I cannot arrest a man for knocking on your door. Maybe he just wanted to borrow some sugar."

"I don't think so, Lieutenant. A man that sour wouldn't have any use for sugar. If you'd seen the way he's acted when he's met me in the hall, you'd know he wouldn't ask me for sugar—or anything else. I'm telling you, he could hardly bear being in the same lobby with me. He'd swerve over to the other side of the hall as though he were afraid he'd get contaminated if he came too close. No, Lieutenant, Mr. Oliphant was hardly neighborly enough to come borrowing sugar. And don't you think it odd that he glared at Kathleen Windsor and my aunt just before they were murdered? And he was seen at St. Simon's Church and you said you thought the killer was a member of the church."

There was a long pause at the other end of the line before the detective spoke again, in the same soft, carefully modulated voice.

"I agree that the man's conduct is peculiar—and from our point of view, interesting. I am glad you called, mademoiselle. I only wished to point out that we cannot arrest a man without some cause. We'll do a little quiet checking on Mr. Oliphant. We will find out if he is a member of St. Simon's Church, what he does for a living, whether he has a criminal record. We'll question the people who know him. It is amazing how the jigsaw puzzle of a person's personality fits together when one talks to people who have seen him in different roles—or wearing different masks, if you will: the mask of the friend, the employee, the patient, the customer, the parishioner. And if what we learn of Mr. Oliphant warrants it, we'll have a little talk with the man himself."

I breathed a sigh of relief. Lieutenant Philippe was taking me seriously after all. But it was going to take time and what if Oliphant came knocking on my door tomorrow night? "Lieutenant, all this investigating is going to take a lot of time, isn't it?"

"No, mademoiselle. I'll put a couple of men on it Monday and in a matter of days we can find out a great deal about your man."

"Do you think it's possible that he's the murderer?"

The detective sounded discouraged. "Who can say? But your neighbor is calling attention to himself by his behavior —and we are going to give him the attention he is asking for. There are four unsolved murders in your district and we can't ignore any possibilities."

"Then you haven't come up with any leads at all?"

158

His voice was weary. "A few, but when we track them down they end in blind alleys. We are not even sure if we are dealing with one murderer or several. George Matrai is still a prime suspect in the Windsor case, but he's vanished without leaving a trace. Remember, he has served time for indecent assault and Kathleen Windsor had been assaulted. And we have discovered another motive for murder in the Windsor killing."

"But I read in the paper that the police thought all the murders were the work of one man."

"That is the *official* statement of the Homicide Department. We must keep our own counsel if we are not to alert the quarry."

Lieutenant Philippe's voice faded out for a moment and then came back. "I must go, mademoiselle; there is an urgent call for me. Be assured we will thoroughly investigate Mr. Oliphant."

"All right, Lieutenant, but what do I do if he comes knocking at my door again?"

"I would advise you not to open it."

The phone clicked softly in my ear. The detective's parting words had made me feel frightened all over again.

Chapter 25

My conversation with Lieutenant Philippe had gotten the day off to a bad start, but by midafternoon Laura's enthusiasm for the Spanish dance company we were seeing tonight had rubbed off on me and I forgot all about the morning's phone call and T. Oliphant. At five o'clock Laura headed

159

for the bathroom with the warning she would be there awhile and did I want to use it first. I said no, I'd had my beauty treatment last night, and smiled to myself. Laura, no doubt, was going to take extraspecial care with her appearance for Julian. I hadn't seen her so sparkly since the days when Carl was the center of her life. She might speak jokingly of Julian forgetting her, as though she didn't really care, but I thought I detected the sound of wedding bells.

When Laura reappeared an hour later she was all aglow —skin, eyes, hair. Wearing a jade pendant and dangly green jade earrings with her new velvet dress, she looked like something out of a fashion magazine. She glided about like a model for my benefit, smoothing the velvet over her hips with a sensuous touch.

I nodded approvingly. "If Julian can forget you in that dress, he's suffering from amnesia. What time is he picking you up?"

"He should be here in a few minutes. And remember, you and Chris are meeting us at the Club Midnight at eight-thirty. Don't make it any later. We want to have time to talk before the stage show starts. We'll be there ahead of you, so ask the waiter for our table. What time is Chris calling for you?"

"At six-thirty, Laura. And I'd better go and get dressed. We'll see you at eight-thirty."

"Right, Nicky. I'm sure you'll love the Felipe Negrete Spanish Ballet. They've been getting wonderful reviews. There's the door now. See you later."

I retreated to the bathroom and made short work of brushing my hair and putting on make-up. Chris didn't like to be kept waiting. I'd decided on wearing my black pant suit with a white lacy blouse and I was just putting on the jacket when the buzzer sounded. I gave my hair another quick brush and went to answer the door. I expected it was Chris, of course, but I wasn't taking any chances. I looked through the peephole first. When I opened the door to him, Chris's rugged face lit up in a smile, but I thought he looked tired. He was putting in long days at the typewriter now and I guessed that the responsibility of Donald weighed heavily on him too.

We decided to go to Luigi's Place for an Italian dinner. It was another on our list of inexpensive-but-good-eating restaurants. It was starting to snow when we reached the restaurant and it was snowing harder when we left Luigi's at eight o'clock—a fine wind-driven snow that stung our faces and obscured visibility. For some unknown reason I felt out of sorts and half-wished we were spending the evening at home in front of the fire. I couldn't blame it on the food because the dinner had been excellent and I'd started feeling funny when we left the apartment. Well, we wouldn't be out very late because Julian had to leave for the airport at eleven. Chris was tired and I was sure he wouldn't object to coming home early, and neither would Laura once she'd seen her Spanish ballet. Laura was mad about flamenco.

We arrived at the Club Midnight shortly before eight-thirty. Julian and Laura were there waiting for us and they had a good table, right in front of center stage. We were in the Starlight Room, an intimate midnight-blue room with winking lights set in a black ceiling. In the semi-darkness, faces were indistinct, but I could see the room was crowded. Laura and Julian greeted us gaily and Julian and Chris shook hands.

"Is it still snowing?" Julian asked Chris. "I'm a little worried about my plane."

"It's coming down hard and there's a driving wind behind it that makes for poor visibility."

Julian got up from the table. "I think I'd better check with the airport and see if the flight's still on."

He was back a few minutes later with the bad news. All flights out of Montreal had been canceled. Julian looked upset and Laura looked pleased.

"I heard the weather report tonight, dear. The storm will be over late tonight and they'll probably put you on a flight

161

tomorrow morning. A few hours one way or the other doesn't matter much, does it?"

"No, I suppose not, Laura." Julian turned to me, his gracious self again. "What will you and Chris have to drink?"

Chris ordered a scotch and soda and I asked for a manhattan. While we were waiting for the drinks Chris was paged. There was an important telephone call for him. He frowned as he got up to follow the waiter. "That must be Donald. He's the only one who knows where I am."

When he came back five minutes later, Chris's frown had become a scowl. "It was Donald and he's all upset. The police went to the apartment tonight and hassled him. And they promised me they'd leave him alone. Now he's afraid they'll come back again."

"But Chris," I asked, "what do they want with him? He told them he didn't know anything about Tony Bartha."

"Well, it looks like they don't believe him. They grilled him about Tony for an hour. And they made sure I was out of the apartment before they went over. I'd like to get my hands on that lantern-jawed detective from the Narcotics Squad. I hope you don't mind, Nicky, but I'll have to go home and calm Donald down. He's scared stiff."

"Of course, Chris," I said, feeling almost as furious as he did over the harassment of Donald. Didn't they have anything better to do than pick on kids?

"Take care of my girl, will you, Julian?" Chris flung the words over his shoulder and was gone, his big frame weaving swiftly between the crowded tables. I sort of wished I was going with him. I didn't feel good at all. And half an hour and one drink later the mystery of what was wrong with me was solved. The tip-off came when I suddenly had trouble seeing Laura and Julian clearly. Little bits of their faces were missing. And then I knew. Migraine. The blurred vision was a forerunner of a migraine headache. I had an attack three or four times a year and I knew that after my sight blurred, a violent headache and nausea followed in swift succession.

162

I was in for a bad time unless I got home quickly and took the pills the doctor had prescribed for me. Miserably I turned to Laura.

"I'm sorry to break up the party, but I'll have to go home. I've got a migraine. If Julian will get a taxi—"

"Oh, Nicky, I'm sorry. You're going to miss a wonderful performance. But we can't let you go home alone like that." Laura turned to Julian. "She gets them occasionally and is as sick as the proverbial dog with them. It gets worse as it goes along unless she takes her pills."

Julian looked concerned—or I thought he looked concerned. I couldn't see him clearly and my head was beginning to pound.

"I'll manage, Laura, if Julian will put me in a cab." I got up a little unsteadily and bumped into the table next to us.

"I say, Laura, I'm afraid we'll have to go. We can't let Nicky go home alone in a taxi when she can't even see properly.

"No," I protested. "Laura loves Spanish dancing and I'm not going to ruin her evening for her."

Julian turned to Laura. "Supposing I take Nicky home and you stay here, Laura? It won't take long to get to your apartment from here. I'll be back in half an hour and you won't miss the beginning of the show."

Laura sounded doubtful. "Will you be all right at home alone, Nicky?"

"Don't worry about me. Once I've had the migraine pills, the symptoms start to let up in half an hour. You stay here and enjoy the performance."

Julian got up and took my arm. "I'll ask the headwaiter to look after you, Laura, and I'll be back in thirty minutes." He beckoned the captain of waiters and explained the situation to him. Then he was guiding me through the maze of tables, out of the Starlight Room and into the checkroom for our coats. When we reached the street we were immersed in a cold whirling sea of snow, whipped by a gale-force wind.

163

Julian led me back inside the entrance to the Club Midnight and told me he'd come back for me when he'd found a taxi. I thought we might be in for a long wait on a night like this. But we were lucky. He was back only a few minutes later. And then, thankfully we were out of the blinding, stinging white mist and on our way home. My head was throbbing rhythmically now and waves of nausea washed over me as we moved bumper to bumper through the slowed-down traffic on Decarie's Sunset Strip. Julian patted my hand in sympathy and assured me we'd be home soon. That's all I could think of now—home and the precious migraine pills. And then a frightening thought insinuated itself into my mind. I would be alone in the apartment tonight. What would I do if T. Oliphant came knocking at my door again? Now I wished Laura had come home with me. I was frightened, deathly frightened, of that strange man who lived down the hall from us. If only the police hadn't gone after Donald tonight. Chris would have brought me home and stayed with me until Laura got home. Wretchedly I slumped against the leather upholstery of the seat, trying to divert my mind from the subject of T. Oliphant. The pain in my head helped. It was hard to concentrate on any subject long with the sickening, pulsing pain in my head. But oh, how I wished Chris were with me tonight.

It seemed to take forever, but finally we were home and Julian was leading me up the front steps and into our apartment building. I fumbled in my purse for my keys and found them by touch. I made an attempt to fit the key into the lock, but with my blurred vision I kept missing the keyhole. Julian took the keys from me and opened the door.

"You're home now, Nicky," he said gently, guiding me to a chair in the hall. He removed my wet coat and hung it in the hall cupboard. I bent down to pull off my boots and with the bending came a wave of nausea and dizziness. I swayed in my chair. Julian caught me and steadied me. The steadying hands on my shoulders moved to my throat.

"Julian," I said, "what are you . . . Julian!" And then my voice was cut off. Julian was throttling me. His voice sounded far way.

"It's too bad you had to get interested in China clippers, Nicky. That was your aunt's mistake."

In terror and disbelief I stared into the face of the strangler. The lips were compressed in a thin, cruel line. The gray-green eyes as cold as a winter sea. There was no mercy in them.

Wildly I thrashed around in the chair, beating at the iron hands around my throat, trying to scream, trying to scream through a windpipe that had been choked off. There was a rushing noise in my ears and the face above me was dissolving in mist. The rushing noise became a roar. Julian's face disappeared. And suddenly I could breathe. I gulped in a great draft of air. Then I was falling, falling into a well of blackness.

Chapter 26

Slowly I floated back to the surface, hearing before I saw. The sounds of a scuffle, shouting, glass breaking. Then there was light. Dazedly I looked at the scene in front of me. Julian Brooks stood in the center of the living room, flanked by two policemen. Blood was running from the corner of his mouth and his hands were manacled. Beside me stood Lieutenant Philippe with a restraining hand on Chris's arm. In a corner Laura stood motionless as a statue, her face a white blur. The coffee table was overturned and broken glass and cigarette ashes littered the floor. Chris was breathing heavily, his fists

165

clenched. Lieutenant Philippe spoke quietly, but there was a commanding edge in his tone.

"I understand your feelings, Mr. Galloway, but we must leave justice to the law."

"All right, Lieutenant," Chris growled, "you can let go of me. I won't hit the bastard again."

I struggled into a sitting position and in a moment Chris was beside me, a supporting arm around me. "You're all right, Muffet, thank God, you're all right!"

I leaned my throbbing head against his shoulder, too sick and shocked to say anything. Julian raised his manacled hands and wiped blood from his mouth.

The detective spoke to the policemen. "Take him down to the car. I'll be down soon."

There was a sneer on Julian's face as the two policemen led him out.

Lieutenant Philippe's blurry bloodhound face was in front of me. "You will be all right, mademoiselle. I will get a doctor for you."

There was something important I had to tell Lieutenant Philippe. At first I could make no sound; then my voice came out in a whisper. "He said it was—"

"Do not try to talk now, mademoiselle. Just rest."

"It's important," I whispered, and the detective bent his head toward me to hear. "When he tried to . . . to strangle me . . . he said it was too bad I got interested in China clippers . . . that was my aunt's mistake."

Chris swore softly. "Does that mean, Lieutenant, that that bastard killed her Aunt Emily?"

"I think so, M. Galloway. I think we have the killer of Emily Teasdale, and possibly Kathleen Windsor as well. Where is the phone, please? I am going to call a doctor for Mlle. Nugent."

Chris led him out of the room and I heard him dialing in the hall. A minute later Laura was beside me with a glass of

166

water and a pillow. She put the pillow at the end of the sofa and slipped something into my hand.

"For your migraine, Nicky." Her voice was low and expressionless.

I took the pills thankfully and Laura held the glass steady in my hand while I drank. Then Chris eased me gently down on the pillow. "Just lie and rest until the doctor gets here, Muffet."

I lay trembling on the sofa, my eyes shut against the light, thinking how wonderful it was to breathe. Lieutenant Philippe was talking to Laura.

"I know you do not feel up to questioning tonight, mademoiselle, and I can wait for a statement from you. Just one thing I would like to know now. Did you give money to Julian Brooks?"

Her voice was whispery. "Yes, I did, Lieutenant."

"How much did you give him?"

"Fifty thousand."

I heard Laura in amazement, too sick and bewildered to try and puzzle anything out tonight.

"We will see that you get it back, Mlle. Prescott."

The door buzzer sounded and a minute later a dark-haired man was standing in front of me, scrutinizing me.

"Do you want me to take her to her bedroom?" Chris asked the doctor.

The voice was authoritative. "Yes, take her to her bed. I'm going to put her to sleep."

Then Chris was carrying me down the hall, depositing me carefully on my bed. "Chris," I whispered, feeling my bruised throat.

"Don't talk now, Nicky. Tomorrow . . . tomorrow we'll sort everything out."

A few minutes later, under the doctor's gentle ministrations, I was drifting off to sleep, the pain in my skull fading away like the room and the blurry face of the doctor.

167

Chapter 27

I slept until nearly ten o'clock Sunday morning under the sedative the doctor had given me. Slowly I got out of bed, feeling weak and shaky after my migraine attack and the attempt on my life last night. When I looked in the bathroom mirror I saw the ugly blue bruises on my throat and shuddered. The events of last night were fantastic, incomprehensible. Charming, well-bred Julian Brooks had tried to kill me. He had killed Aunt Emily. Incredible to think that if Chris and the police had arrived thirty seconds later last night I would have been Julian's second victim—or possibly his third. I couldn't understand anything at all. What had brought Chris and the police to the apartment right on our heels? What had been the tip-off? What did Julian mean about China clippers? Why had he tried to kill me? Why had he killed Aunt Emily?

I didn't feel like getting dressed, but I supposed the police would be down with their questions, so I pulled on a pair of suede pants and a turtleneck sweater to hide the marks on my throat. Laura's bedroom door was closed, which meant she was still in bed. I moved quietly in the kitchen in order not to waken her. Poor Laura would waken soon enough to the shocking reality that had hit her last night. The man she loved was a murderer. And she had handed over her bank account to him! I couldn't imagine level-headed, businesslike Laura doing such a wild thing. How had he gotten it out of her?

I didn't have much of an appetite and my breakfast consisted of a glass of orange juice and two cups of coffee. Then I went to call Chris. An envelope was lying on the floor of the hall just in front of the door. I picked it up, wondering what it was doing there. It was a letter addressed to me from a friend in Vancouver. Attached to the letter was a scrap of paper fastened with a paper clip. "The mailman left this in my box —T. Oliphant," it read. So that's why our neighbor had come to my door Friday night. He had a letter for me! And here I'd been imagining that T. Oliphant had come to the apartment to strangle me! Normally I would have laughed at the humor in the situation, but today I was too shaken and stunned by last night's events to find anything even remotely humorous.

I dialed Chris's number, feeling a sudden savage surge of hatred toward Julian Brooks well up in me. Chris answered the phone on the second ring, his voice eager.

"I've been sitting by the phone wondering if you were up yet. How are you this morning, Nicky?"

"Not so good, Chris. I'm so shocked by what happened last night I feel as though I've been hit by a freight train."

"I can imagine, and I'll bet Laura feels like she's been hit by the locomotive. Seeing them together last night at the Club Midnight, I had the feeling she was carrying a torch for Brooks. How is she taking it?"

"She's not up yet. I'm letting her sleep as long as she can. She's going to take it hard. Chris, how did you *know* last night?"

"I'm coming down to see you now and I'll tell you what I can. We'll have to wait for that detective to get the whole story. He told me last night he wants to talk to you and Laura today if you're feeling up to it. He said it could wait another day if you'd rather."

"I don't feel much like talking and I don't suppose Laura does either, but I'd like to get it over with. Did he say he'd phone?"

"I said I'd see how you were and phone him from your place. See you in half an hour, Nicky."

Chris arrived at eleven-thirty, sweeping me into an embrace

169

in the hall that lifted me off my feet. Then he set me down gently, stood back and looked me over. "You look a little wan, but you'll do, Muffet, you'll do," he said gruffly. With his arm around me, he walked me into the living room to the sofa. He sat down beside me and never had the big guy with the thoughtful blue eyes and the cleft in his chin looked so beautiful to me as he did that morning after my brush with death.

He looked at me soberly. "What, exactly, did Julian say to you last night about China clippers?"

"We'd just gotten in, Chris, and Julian started strangling me. He said, 'It's too bad you had to get interested in China clippers, Nicky. That was your aunt's mistake.' "

"So it was our gentlemanly Julian Brooks who murdered your Aunt Emily. I should have killed him when I had my hands on him last night. And he thought *you* had the sketch!"

"What sketch?"

"Let me begin at the beginning, or as near the beginning as I can. Remember I was down here the night after Kathleen Windsor's murder? You were sick with the flu so we didn't go out for dinner as we'd planned?"

"Yes, I remember."

"You had just read of the murder in the paper and were pretty upset about it. Well, you left the living room to get some aspirin and I noticed a piece of sheet music on your coffee table. It was called 'A Rap with the Lord' and had Kathleen Windsor's name on it. I figured right away that she'd left it at your place the night before when she came here after being followed from choir practice. I was also pretty sure you hadn't noticed the music on the table and that seeing a visible reminder of her in your apartment might upset you some more. Anyway, I put the song in my coat pocket and took it home with me. I was wearing an old jacket that Saturday and haven't worn it since, so there was nothing to remind me of the music until last night. Then, in the Club Midnight, when Julian went to phone the airport about his flight, I saw a draw-

170

ing on a piece of paper at his place at the table. It was a drawing of a sailing ship done in red ink and it reminded me of the sketch I'd seen on the cover of 'A Rap with the Lord.' I was almost sure those two drawings had been done by the same hand. If that was so, it meant Julian Brooks knew Kathleen Windsor . . . knew her well enough to doodle on her music. There had been some talk that Kathleen had had a boy friend, but the police hadn't been able to find a trace of a man in her life. And here was a link-up between Kathleen and Julian. I pocketed the sketch, intending to compare it with the one on the murdered woman's music when I got home. I was hoping Julian wouldn't notice the paper was gone. Donald's phone call drove everything else out of mind. But it didn't take long to calm him down once I'd gotten home. Just having me there reassured him. Then I compared the sketch on 'A Rap with the Lord' with the one I'd picked up at the Club Midnight. It was the same ship—with a figurehead of an angel blowing a trumpet at the bow. Both drawings were approximately the same scale, done in the same vermilion ink, with the same thick strokes. There was no doubt in my mind that Julian had made both drawings. So far as I knew, he hadn't breathed a word of knowing Kathleen Windsor, but he had known her well enough to draw on her choir music. I decided to get hold of your detective right away. I got his home phone number by telling headquarters it was urgent. Philippe was in—and very interested. He said he was going to do a little checking and would call me back. When he phoned ten minutes later he was excited. He had called Brooks's hotel and had been told that he had checked out that afternoon, leaving a Vancouver forwarding address. And Brooks had told Laura he was going to Rome for a few days on business. Lieutenant Philippe figured he was on the run and they'd better nab him fast. He couldn't get out of the city that night with the storm, but he could well get on an early-morning flight to somewhere—and not necessarily Rome. Philippe was sure Brooks wouldn't tell Laura where he was really

171

headed for. The detective said he was on his way to the Club Midnight with a couple of constables and I figured I'd better go along to look after you girls. I got there at the same time as the police and Laura informed us you'd taken sick and Julian had gone home with you. We hightailed it to your place and got here just as Brooks went into his strangling routine. When he heard the key in the lock he made a run for the balcony door to the lane but didn't quite make it. And it was the weary Lieutenant Philippe who brought him down with a flying tackle. You were lying in a heap in the hall and I was ready to take Brooks apart."

"But I still don't understand, Chris. Why did he try to kill *me?*"

"It's tied in with that drawing of a clipper ship. Julian must have thought *you* saw the drawing on Kathleen Windsor's music. He knew she came here from choir practice the night she was murdered. And he was afraid you'd taken that paper at the Club Midnight to compare the two. He didn't suspect me of taking the paper because he didn't know I'd seen the music. I'm going to call Philippe now. Are you sure you want to talk to him today?"

"Yes, the sooner it's over with, the better. I'm sure Laura feels the same way."

While Chris was talking on the phone I heard Laura moving about in the kitchen. When I went out to talk to her she was sitting in the breakfast nook with a cup of coffee in front of her. The face that had been all aglow last night was pale and drawn-looking, the green eyes lifeless. When she spoke, her voice was as flat and lifeless as her eyes.

"How are you this morning, Nicky?"

"Not too good. But I'll be all right in another day. You really loved the guy, didn't you, Laura?"

Her voice was very low. "Yes, I did. I loved a swine."

"I'm so sorry, Laura."

"Don't worry about me, I'll survive; but you can bet I'll never be taken in again. From now on I travel alone."

172

There was nothing I could say that would help Laura right now. I could only hope that time would heal the wound. "You told Lieutenant Philippe last night that you'd given Julian fifty thousand dollars—"

"Wait until the police get here and you'll hear all about it." There was a bitter twist to her mouth. "I don't want to have to tell the story twice of what a fool I was."

Chris walked into the kitchen in time to hear this last remark. He looked at Laura with compassion in his eyes. Then he spoke to both of us. "Lieutenant Philippe is a very busy man today, but he says he can make it down about four o'clock and he'd like to talk to both of you."

"Chris," I asked, still finding it hard to believe, "did Julian confess to killing Aunt Emily?"

"The lieutenant wouldn't go into any detail. Just said they expected to have a confession in a couple of hours. Apparently Julian's been getting a lot of attention from the police since they arrested him. Supposing I make everybody lunch and then you girls can go rest until Philippe gets here. I'll go out for a walk and read for a while."

"Whatever you like, Chris, but don't come up with submarine sandwiches. I haven't much appetite and I don't think Laura has either."

We ended up having soup and toasted tomato sandwiches in an atmosphere reminiscent of a funeral home. Then Laura and I went to our rooms and left Chris to his own devices. I was still fuzzy-headed from the sedative I'd been given last night and went off to sleep in minutes. It seemed to me I'd been sleeping just a few minutes when Chris knocked at my door to tell me Lieutenant Philippe was here. A few minutes later the three of us were sitting in the living room with the detective. The bags under his eyes were more pronounced and he sagged against the back of the sofa as though he didn't have the strength to sit up.

"I expected," he said in his soft-spoken voice, "I would have a lot of questions for Mlle. Nugent and Mlle. Prescott. However, M. Brooks has obligingly answered most of them for us. I will not have statements ready for you to sign for a few days, but I came today because I knew you would be anxious to hear the outcome of my long tête-à-tête with M. Brooks."

"Did you get a confession out of him?" Chris asked.

"We did," said the detective. "In fact, we got several."

"What do you mean?" I asked.

"I mean, mademoiselle, that Julian Brooks has confessed to the killing of Elsie Grunberger, Kathleen Windsor and Emily Teasdale."

There was a stunned silence in the room. Laura stared at the lieutenant as though she hadn't heard right. Then Chris swore softly. "All three of them! It's unbelievable! How did you get him to confess? And why did he do it?"

"To answer your first question, M. Galloway, let us go back to last night. M. Brooks thought he was taking a plane trip last night and he brought his bag to the Club Midnight. That bag got special attention at headquarters last night and it was well worth it. We found a false bottom in it. In the real bottom of the bag we found one hundred and fifty thousand dollars in cash, forged identification, a black wig and Vandyke beard, black eyebrows and dark make-up. We had found the black-haired man with the pointy little devil beard Mme. Teasdale had seen Kathleen Windsor with. If that weren't evidence enough, one of the two passports we found bore the name of Steven Harcourt. The photo was of Julian Brooks, a M. Brooks with black hair and a spade beard. One of the diaries we found in Mlle. Windsor's bedroom was devoted to her dark-haired Steven. As she had filled several diaries with outpourings of love for different men, we thought the men involved were products of a love-starved woman's mind. Then, in the course of our investigation, we looked into Mlle. Windsor's financial affairs. We found that her bank account had been depleted by $100,000 in the month preceding her murder. She had made out two checks—in the amount of fifty thousand dollars each—to Steven Harcourt. We started a

174

search for him but couldn't find him. We figured once he had gotten the money from Mlle. Windsor, he had left the city. These men who prey on women do not stay long in one place. We still did not think that Harcourt had murdered Kathleen Windsor. Her murder looked like the work of a sexual deviate. But what Brooks said last night to Mlle. Nugent about her Aunt Emily made me immediately suspicious. He had as much as admitted that he had strangled Emily Teasdale. And if he had strangled one woman, it seemed possible that he had strangled another.

"The doorman at Mlle. Windsor's apartment house told me a dark-haired man with a beard had entered the building about ten after twelve the night the Windsor woman was murdered. The doorman was late going off duty for the night and didn't pay much attention to the man he passed going out, but he said he thought he would recognize him if he saw him again. We persuaded M. Brooks to become Steven Harcourt. He was a little reluctant to put on the beard and wig, but as I say, we persuaded him. Then we put him in a police lineup. The doorman pointed him out immediately, even though we had another man in the lineup with dark hair and a beard. We confronted Brooks with the doorman. With the doorman's identification of him, he started to crack. We told him we knew he killed the Windsor woman and we knew he killed Emily Teasdale. We then produced a man who testified he saw Brooks leaving Mme. Teasdale's apartment between six-fifteen and six-twenty-five the night she was murdered. We made the time indefinite because, of course, our witness hadn't seen Brooks at all. Unfair, perhaps, but then, cold-blooded killers know nothing of fairness. With the second identification, our man conceded defeat. He confessed to the three slayings, even boasted about them."

Chris rubbed his jaw thoughtfully. "But I still don't get it. Why did he kill Kathleen Windsor? Why didn't he just beat it once he got her money? And why the Grunberger woman and Nicky's aunt?"

The detective rubbed the pouch under one eye and crossed his legs. "I am coming to that, M. Galloway. It all began with Mlle. Windsor. Charles Potter—we may as well begin calling him by his right name—made her acquaintance at a charity ball held by the Windermere Women's Club. He made a point of attending affairs given by exclusive women's clubs. With his well-bred charm and boyish good looks, Potter made a very favorable impression on Mlle. Windsor. It didn't take him long to get the vital information from his intended victim: She was single and well-to-do. Flattered by his attention, Kathleen Windsor said yes when he asked her to have lunch with him the following Sunday. That was the beginning. They always met somewhere away from Kathleen's apartment and when Potter brought her home he never took her right to Seabury House. He usually left her at the corner of Winnicott and Queen Mary. Kathleen walked the rest of the way alone. She had told Potter her mother would disapprove of her going out with a man and even though her mother was then in the hospital with a broken hip, Kathleen was afraid that someone would see her with Potter and report it to her mother. This suited Charles Potter perfectly. He too was afraid that someone would see him with Kathleen and later identify him, even though he was wearing the guise of Steven Harcourt. He led the woman along until she believed he was in love with her. Then he asked for money. He told her he had the opportunity of buying a furniture plant but had to have the money right away to close the sale. He could pay her back in a month, he told her, from the proceeds of the sale of an apartment building he had just put on the market."

I heard a strangled noise from Laura but didn't dare look at her. Lieutenant Philippe seemed to be making a point of not looking at her either. He went on in his quiet, even voice.

"Mlle. Windsor, all unsuspecting, made out two certified checks for Potter, two weeks apart. The night she gave him the second check he got careless. He drove her right to Seabury House, then got out of the car and escorted her to the

door of the building. A woman came out as they stood talking for a minute at the door. It was Elsie Grunberger, who
sang in St. Simon's choir with Kathleen. Kathleen said hello to
the woman and introduced Potter to her as Steven Harcourt.
Potter took his leave right behind Elsie Grunberger. He recognized her as the friend of a woman in Burlington he'd
fleeced out of her life savings a year ago. He had been pos-
ing as Julian Brooks then with his own blond hair and he was
certain Elsie didn't recognize him with the black hair and
beard. He passed her on Winnicott. Then he slipped on an
icy patch and fell—right under a street light. His black wig
flew off and while Julian retrieved it and got to his feet the
woman stared hard at him, then hurried on. He knew she'd
recognized him and that she would probably call Kathleen
Windsor as soon as she got home. And Potter had still to
cash the check for fifty thousand dollars. The woman had to
be stopped. Potter followed her until they came to a garage
with the door open. He took a quick look around to see if
anybody else was on the street. Then he acted. From behind,
he got a strangle hold on the woman's throat, dragged her
into the garage and throttled her. The car's motor was running and he knew the owner might return any second. He
darted out of the garage, turned the corner into Phoebe
Lane and disappeared in the lane at the end of the street. Potter cashed his certified check the next day. Then he put away
his dark hair pieces and became Julian Brooks. He intended
to fly to Switzerland in a few days, but before he bought his
airline ticket he saw Mlle. Prescott's advertisement in the paper for a restaurant. It was unfortunate that Mlle. Prescott
prefixed her name with the word 'miss' in the advertisement.
It was too much for Potter to resist. A single woman with
enough money to go into the restaurant business. He replied
to her advertisement, his voice disguised, saying he had a delicatessen for sale. He was his usual charming self on the telephone, drawing her out until she'd told him what he wanted
to know. She had fifty thousand dollars to invest in the busi-

ness. Potter thought it was worth going after. Mlle. Prescott made an appointment to see the restaurant on a Saturday at three. Potter was there, sitting in a booth at the front of the restaurant near the cashier's desk. He was wearing his wig and beard. While the bewildered Mlle. Prescott patiently explained to the equally bewildered owner that he'd answered her advertisement, Potter took Miss Prescott in, registering every detail of her appearance. She would be easy to spot with her red hair and white suede coat and boots. Filing Mlle. Prescott's picture away in memory, Potter then decided the next step was to murder the Windsor woman. He would be in Montreal a few months longer after all and had to prevent her from raising a hue and cry when she discovered that not only her money but her loved one had disappeared. Knowing that the doorman went off duty at midnight, Potter went to her apartment at ten after twelve, in his guise of Steven Harcourt. He spoke to Kathleen over the intercom system, giving some plausible excuse for calling so late. Mlle. Windsor admitted him, of course, and five minutes later she was dead. Potter then partly disrobed her to make it look as though she had been sexually molested. He hoped the police would conclude the woman was murdered by a sexual deviate and look no further for a motive. And this is exactly what we did at first. But when the strangling murders continued we decided to dig deeper."

Laura, who had been gazing into space, seemingly oblivious of everything around her, turned her stricken eyes on the detective. "That attack on me in the park . . . was that set up?"

"Yes, Mlle. Prescott. Potter knew you wouldn't be as easy to con as Mlle. Windsor. He couldn't count on your falling for his brand of flattery right off. He had to think of another way to interest you, to hold you to him. The resourceful Potter came up with a staged attack on you, with himself in the role of rescuer. He knew this would gain your gratitude, create a bond that would make you vulnerable to his attentions. It was easy to set up. Mlle. Prescott, in her telephone conversation

178

with the supposed restaurant owner, had told Potter she attended restaurant administration classes on Mondays and Thursdays at the Drummond Business Institute. He had also elicited from her the useful information that she didn't drive her car in the winter. M. Potter found out what time the classes ended and on the Monday after Kathleen Windsor's murder he was sitting parked in a car in front of the institute. Of course a lot depended on chance. Mlle. Prescott might get a drive home with someone. She might not even be at her class that night, but luck was with Potter. He spotted her easily coming out of the building in her all-white outfit. And she was alone. He got out of his car and followed her at a distance. When Potter saw her take up her stand at a 62 bus stop, he went back to his car. Then, knowing what route she was taking home, he drove to the bus stop a block from her street and parked on the other side of the road. In the back of the car was a disreputable individual known to the police as Lido. Potter had briefed him well. When Mlle. Prescott got off her bus, Lido slipped out of the car and followed her. Potter was driving slowly behind him watching for pedestrians. Luck was with him again. The street was deserted. In front of the park, Lido staged his attack, Potter jumped out of his car and dashed into the park after them, putting Mlle. Prescott's assailant to flight. The outcome was as our man expected. Mlle. Prescott saw Potter in the role of Knight in Shining Armor and was immediately attracted to him. Then the Knight set himself up in a prestigious apartment and rented a prestigious car to give the impression he was well-heeled.

"Potter played it carefully with Mlle. Prescott. When he was sure her gratitude toward him had changed to love, he offhandedly remarked that he had the opportunity of a lifetime to buy a furniture plant at half its value. Ruefully he added that if the chance had come a little later he'd have been able to grab it. He was negotiating the sale of an apartment building and the transaction would be completed in a month. But the owner wanted cash right away as he was leaving the country and he had another prospective buyer who said he could raise the cash in two weeks. Potter did not even have to ask for the money. Mlle. Prescott offered to lend it to him without any qualms. After all, it would only be for a month."

Laura spoke bitterly. "He was such a gentleman. Said he couldn't take money from a woman. I had to *persuade* him to take it. He asked me to please not mention it to anyone because he felt so embarrassed about it! And he spoke so knowledgeably about plastics and designing, he had me completely fooled. I believed everything he told me."

There was a hint of pity in Lieutenant Philippe's cynical gray eyes as he looked at Laura. "As I said before, M. Potter was a resourceful man. He boasted he could pass himself off as anything he wanted to. For his role of furniture designer he simply read a few copies of *Canadian Interieurs* and *The Home Goods Market* to learn the jargon of the trade. But to finish the story, on Friday Potter cashed the fifty-thousand-dollar check Mlle. Prescott had given him and made arrangements to leave the city yesterday. And incidentally, he was booked on a flight to Zurich, Switzerland, not Rome. Conveniently, he had a numbered account in Switzerland. He intended to stay there a few months and then go hunting again. And if it hadn't been that Potter loved boats almost as much as money, he'd be in Switzerland today. We found a folder full of sketches of China clippers in his luggage. At every opportunity for doodling, he sketched a sailing ship. Unfortunately for him, he sketched the *Flying Cloud* twice too often. Did M. Galloway tell you how we were put on to Potter last night?"

"Chris told me this morning," I said, "but Laura didn't hear the story."

For Laura's benefit, the detective told of how Chris had connected the sketch on Kathleen Windsor's music with the sketch Julian had made at the Club Midnight and alerted the police. She listened silently, her head down. Then she spoke in that low, expressionless voice that chilled me.

180

"But why did he kill Mrs. Teasdale and why did he go after Nicky?"

"He killed Mme. Teasdale because she had seen the sketch on 'A Rap with the Lord.' Do you recall the night that Mme. Teasdale came down with the two boys to pick up a birthday cake?"

"I remember," I said. "Chris and I were going out with two friends to see a play and Laura was going out with Julian. And I remember something about a sketch now, Lieutenant. Julian drew a sailing ship on a piece of paper while he was waiting for Laura. Chris hadn't arrived yet. Aunt Emily picked the drawing up and commented that it was a pretty ship and she'd seen one just like it somewhere. Julian said she had probably seen a drawing of a ship like it at the Warwick Tearoom. There were sketches of China clippers on one wall."

"Exactly, mademoiselle, and what did your Aunt Emily say when Potter said this?"

"Let me think . . . she said something . . . I know . . . she said, yes, that's where she'd seen a picture like it. She said something else . . . oh yes, she said the tearoom had sketches of sailing ships done in red ink."

"Yes," said Lieutenant Philippe grimly, "and with those words Mme. Teasdale signed her death warrant. At the time Potter thought that his sketch had reminded your aunt of ones she'd seen in the tearoom. But two days later, a thought struck him. The sketches in the Warwick Tearoom were of British clippers. The sketch he'd made two days before at your apartment had been of the *Flying Cloud,* an American clipper with the figurehead of an angel blowing a trumpet. None of the British clippers had a figurehead like that. Yet Mme. Teasdale had said she'd seen one just like it. Then she had said the drawings in the tearoom were done in red ink. They weren't. They were black and white sketches. Potter was puzzled at first. Then he recalled that he'd drawn a sketch of the *Flying Cloud* in red ink on Kathleen Windsor's choir music a few weeks previously. And Miss Nugent had told him

181

that her Aunt Emily sang in the choir and was talking to Kathleen Windsor after practice the night she was murdered. It hit Potter like a blow. Mme. Teasdale had seen the sketch on 'A Rap with the Lord.' But she hadn't *remembered* where she'd seen a drawing like the one Julian Brooks—or rather Potter—made at your place the night she was there. She snatched at Potter's explanation that it was probably at the Warwick Tearoom. Potter figured that sooner or later your aunt would recall where she'd *really* seen a drawing like the one he'd sketched that Friday night at your apartment— and then Potter would be linked with Kathleen Windsor. He wasn't about to clear out of Montreal when there was a prize of fifty thousand dollars to be gained from Mlle. Prescott. Cold-bloodedly he decided to silence Mme. Teasdale before her memory improved. She had mentioned where she lived the last night she was here with Potter, so there was no problem. He went calling on Mme. Teasdale that fatal Sunday at six-fifteen. She, of course, welcomed the nice young man who'd been at her niece's the previous Friday. A few minutes later she had been silenced forever. Potter got out of the building unseen, congratulating himself on his cleverness. Then he made the mistake of sketching a clipper ship last night at the Club Midnight. When he came back to the table after phoning the airport and discovered that the paper with the sketch on it was missing, he suspected something right away. Why would anyone take the paper without telling him? He reasoned that Mlle. Nugent too had seen the sketch he'd made on the Windsor woman's sheet music. The murdered woman had been here after choir practice the night she was killed and of course she would have had her music with her. He jumped to the conclusion that Mlle. Nugent recognized the drawing and was going to the police with it. When Mlle. Nugent became ill last night and said she had to go home, Potter thought she was putting on an act to get away and phone the police. Now Mlle. Nugent had to be silenced. And you all know the rest of the story."

182

"What a ruthless devil," Chris said grimly. "And you stopped me from hitting him!"

"The Law will take care of Potter, M. Galloway. I promise you, the Law will take good care of him."

"But what about that fourth killing—the Cassidy woman. Was Potter responsible for that one too?"

"No, mademoiselle, Potter did not kill Eileen Cassidy. We still have to solve that one. But today we solved three out of four. Not a bad day's work for a Sunday."

The detective got up wearily, his long bloodhound face a study in melancholy. He turned to Laura. "I will have a statement ready for you to sign in a few days, mademoiselle, and do not worry about your money. It will be returned to you shortly."

Laura nodded, her face blank of expression, and Chris and I accompanied the detective to the door. He shrugged into his coat, set his dilapidated gray hat on the back of his head, bowed, and was gone.

Chapter 28

A month has passed since that fateful Saturday when the mask was ripped off Julian Brooks and the face of the foe revealed. Lieutenant Philippe says he will stand trial for the murder of Kathleen Windsor only. As the detective said dryly, they can only hang him once. But hanging Charles Potter won't bring Aunt Emily or Kathleen Windsor or Elsie Grunberger back to life. It won't mend Laura's shattered dream. She's trying to pick up the pieces, throwing herself heart and soul into her restaurant project. It's all she's got now. But I still have hopes for Laura. As I said before, she's too much of a woman to go through life without a man.

Donald Hammill is now living in a supervised apartment house for teen-aged boys. He's busy and happy spinning disks all day in a music store and practicing the accordion at night with missionary fervor. He's got to be ready to perform when Laura's restaurant opens in May. My big, tough Chris said he was glad to get the boy off his hands. He just *happens* to be in the neighborhood of Donald's home now and then and drops in to see how he's doing.

I still don't like T. Oliphant, but at least I'm not afraid of him now. Lieutenant Philippe did a little checking on him and the report he had for me was reassuring. Theodore Oliphant, the detective told me, was an eccentric who did not like women. But he had never harmed one and wasn't likely to do so. He just avoided them. Children, however, were a different story. Our next-door neighbor, in his peculiar, shy way, loves children. He makes simple educational toys in his apartment and donates many of them to children's hospitals and orphanages. So much for Mr. Oliphant's bomb-making activities. Sybil Hepworth was going to be disappointed when she learned what he did for a living. I decided I wouldn't be the one to tell her. Why take the excitement out of her life?

The mystery of where Guy Sabourin got the money to make his luxury purchases is solved. It all came out when he went to work one morning driving his Mercedes-Benz and came home at night driving a modestly priced compact. Lisa asked questions of course and Guy finally admitted he'd had to sell his expensive car to raise money. It took some time to get the whole story out of Guy, but he finally broke down and confessed that he had been gambling. He had beginner's luck at first and won fifteen thousand dollars without half trying. Elated and confident that he'd found a way to make easy money, Guy had rushed out and bought a prestige car and a mink for Lisa. His beginner's luck soon changed, but Guy didn't know when to call it quits. Now he owes five thousand

184

dollars and is working overtime to earn the title of top salesman of the year. Guy is counting on the bonus awarded to put
him back on his feet financially. I don't think Guy Sabourin
will ever get over his need for ostentatious display, but maybe
with wise feet-on-the-ground Lisa beside him to set an example, it can be toned down a little.

Chris is in rare good humor these days. It may be because
he got his book finished just under the deadline and can relax
and take a brief holiday from writing. Or it may be because
we're getting married in April. I made up my mind to say
yes to Chris the night Charles Potter tried to kill me. I had to
look into the face of death before I understood how precious
life was. That was my moment of truth. When the cruel hands
cut off my oxygen supply and my starving lungs seemed about
to burst . . . when a wind roared in my head and life fal-
tered—then I knew how much I wanted to live. It seems
strange to me now that I dithered and dallied so long before
giving Chris an answer. Because it's all so crystal-clear now.
Life is too precious to be half-lived. It has to be lived wholeheartedly, passionately, with all one's being. And it has to be
lived *now*—because who knows if tomorrow will ever come.
I decided to do what Chris suggested—take the leap of faith.
I can only land in his arms. And I'm not afraid now of en-
circling arms—of surrender to something bigger than myself.
I'm no longer afraid of being caught up, drowned in the surg-
ing eddies of my love for Christopher Galloway. I'm willing
to take chances now. I'm willing to make the descent into the
whirlpool, trusting I'll surface safely with Chris by my side.
And I've given up my resentment of Chris's love affair with a
typewriter. I grew up a lot that terrifying night in January
when life was nearly taken from me. I was a greedy, possessive
child who wanted to have her cake and eat it too. Now I know
it's enough to be alive. I don't have to own anyone. I've accepted Chris's writing career and all it entails. I know there'll
be times I'll feel shut out, excluded, when he's in the throes of
producing a book, but I'm not going to make a memorandum

185

of it. As long as I have his heart, I'm not going to be jealous of the fictional people who have his head.

The snow lies deep on the graves of Kathleen Windsor and Aunt Emily, but I like to think that somewhere beyond the blue Kathleen Windsor is happily rapping with the Lord and Aunt Emily is vroooming down celestial highways, pockets bulging with provender for heavenly birds and animals.